Praise for L

Welcome to your new favorite YA sci-fi series! *Landfall: The Ship Series Book One* hurls us into a frightening and fascinating future rich with action, mystery, and unforgettable characters. With elements of Orson Scott Card's Ender's Game and the best of Rick Riordan's Percy Jackson books, Landfall kept me burning through the pages. I hope Jerry Aubin is typing right now, because I can't wait to return to The Ship!

- Owen Egerton, author of *Hollow*

RENDEZVOUS

THE SHIP SERIES // BOOK FOUR

JERRY AUBIN

For any information, please contact zax@theshipseries.com.

The main text of this book was set in Georgia.
The chapter title text was set in Avenir.

Lekanyane Publishing
Austin // Amsterdam // Cape Town // Sydney // Christchurch

ISBN 978-0-9970708-7-3 (pbk)
ISBN 978-0-9970708-6-6 (ebk)

For K, P, W, and Q.

THE STORY SO FAR...

LANDFALL introduces us to Zax and Kalare, two cadets approaching their sixteenth birthdays, as they work to establish their careers in the Ship's Crew. The two catch the eye of the Flight Boss, the second most powerful member of the Omegas running the Ship, and he offers to mentor the one who comes out on top after a series of training competitions. Mikedo, a Flight Lieutenant, leads their instruction and quickly forms deep bonds with the two cadets. The training culminates with a mission to explore a planet prior to colonization where Zax makes a startling discovery— what appears to be a spacecraft built by unknown humans. Mikedo convinces Zax that his discovery is a danger to the Ship's fragile society, and her fears gain credence when she dies under mysterious circumstances shortly thereafter. Zax identifies sufficient circumstantial evidence to suspect the Flight Boss of conspiring to kill Mikedo and hide the discovery of unknown humans, and he publicly confronts the man with it. The Boss laughs off the accusations and punishes Zax by banishing him to the bottom of the Ship's hierarchy.

REVOLUTION picks up one year later with Zax and Kalare moving in two different directions. She has thrived under the Boss's mentorship and loves the Pilot Academy, while he toils in the literal bowels of the Ship serving under the most clueless of its officers. The civilian uprising triggered by Zax's discovery of the human fighter boils over into full revolution. The two cadets, along with Zax's longtime nemesis Aleron, become enmeshed in a mission to help Sergeant Bailee, a fierce Marine, keep the Boss out of the civilians' hands in order to protect the Ship. Along the way, Zax runs afoul of Rege, a leader of the revolutionaries, and shockingly discovers their movement is led by no other than Imair—a civilian woman he had worked side-by-side with for a year. Zax accepts a mission to kill the Boss rather than allow the civilian revolution to succeed, but he fails when the man appears to betray the Crew in order to save himself and remain in power. The Boss rewards Zax and restores him to his position atop the Crew's hierarchy with an appointment to the Pilot Academy, but it is an uneasy truce as Zax continues to believe the man is a murderous traitor.

HOMEWARD opens with a trip back in time and introduces Adan—a brilliant innovator who designs a spacefaring ark to save humanity from Earth's environmental collapse. Along with his fearsome bodyguard and trusted lieutenant Markev, Adan travels to Earth's asteroid belt and returns with a massive space rock that becomes the foundation of the Ship. The Chancellor, the ruthless leader of the West, supports Adan in his efforts, but her cooperation comes at the steep price of Adan's independence. He regretfully compromises even further when he makes a deal with the General Secretary, a foe who has led the

East for decades in its battles against the West, to gain access to the East's consciousness transfer technology that Adan requires for the Ship's powerful fighter craft. Back in Zax's timeline, Imair leads the Ship along with her murderous lieutenant Rege as it starts a twelve-year journey back towards Earth in search of the mysterious humans. Zax's dream of piloting a fighter is finally within reach as he starts his training at the Pilot Academy and meets his new friend Mase—a precocious younger cadet who hacks into the Ship's Artificial Intelligence systems in his spare time. Zax thrives professionally and reaches the top of his Academy class, but his personal life gets thrown into upheaval when Kalare tires of his suspicions about her beloved mentor the Flight Boss and walks away from their friendship. Zax discovers his paranoia about the Boss is well-founded when he learns the officer has hit Zax with enough demerits to get him Culled, and Zax's timeline comes to a close as he descends into cryosleep.

RENDEZVOUS begins with a return to Adan's timeline and shines a light on his adversaries from the East...

CHAPTER ONE

I will once again respectfully decline your invitation.

With a seat out of the camera's view, Rilee didn't have to worry about what her facial expressions might reveal. It was just as well since it was impossible to hide her feelings about the man on the giant video wall. The press may have christened Adan a modern-day Noah on a mission to save the species, but she harbored a deep distrust of the man and his motives. The General Secretary spoke once the connection was established.

"Hello, Adan. How are things progressing?"

"Fine, Mr. Secretary. We've made great progress on the accommodations for your citizens since we last spoke. I've personally overseen the construction to ensure that everything is prepared according to plan."

"We appreciate it, Adan. I have to say that, from everything I've heard, it's been a fantastic experience for everyone on the team to work with you. We greatly appreciate how you've welcomed us into your project."

"It's been my pleasure, Mr. Secretary. I'm quite pleased to know that we'll be able to take care of you and others from your society when we depart."

The Secretary shot a subtle glance to Rilee before replying to Adan with a smile.

"I think that qualifies as the most surprising thing I've ever heard in my one hundred and sixty years."

Adan did a visible double-take up on the screen, and the leader of the East broke out into laughter.

"What—did you legitimately not realize how old I was, Adan? I was already sixty when I was among the first of us who Uploaded. I've allowed my Pattern to age a little through the years that I've been General Secretary to give the appearance I was getting older, but I assumed everyone saw through that charade. Glad to see the effort paid off with at least one casual observer."

"My apologies, Mr. Secretary. But no, I was not aware of how old you are. You've always seemed ageless. I will admit to not having cared enough to pay attention to the fact that you truly are."

"No apologies necessary, Adan. Those of us in the East appreciate how much our lives differ from those of you in the West and how disorienting that can be. You've always associated me with this Pattern and that's fine, but ultimately it's nothing but the design for a uniform I slip into for my job. Sometimes I have different jobs and they require different uniforms. An ease with inhabiting various Skins is as natural for us after a hundred years as breathing is for you. I can hardly imagine what Patterns I might choose from at some point off in the future after you or your descendants have resettled me and my people. Perhaps we'll choose a glorious water planet and live as mermen. Regardless, we have you to thank for the opportunity to survive and we are grateful."

"Your gratitude, sir, is echoed in how all of us up here feel about the contributions of your team. In fact, I really should cut this call off now as I need to prepare for the final verification of their work."

"Thank you, Adan. I will look forward to shaking your hand soon."

The connection went dead and Adan's visage was replaced with an exterior view of his massive spacecraft. The tower being built for the East, started so late in the process, was the only one that still crawled with construction equipment. Rilee couldn't help being impressed with what Adan and the West had accomplished with their asteroid, but the conversation she just witnessed only served to stoke her misgivings. She collected her thoughts and then turned to the Secretary. The man smiled as he waited for her to speak.

"He's playing you, sir."

"I know, Rilee. The question I need you to answer is how. The hair on the back of my neck is up like we're walking into a trap, but no one has a good theory for what it might be."

"It's hard to say, sir. The operational security is rock solid up on that ark of his. He's got all of the workers compartmentalized, so it's impossible to get much of anything useful out of them. They each have such a small view of the overall project that talking to them is like looking through a series of pinholes. The most senior person we tried to extract information from—well, that ended poorly."

"Poorly is the understatement of the year, Rilee. We finally had our hands on someone who might give a peek into what's hidden behind all of Adan's public smiles and platitudes, and your team let her kill herself before you even got started."

Rilee glanced down at the floor for a moment and then met her leader's gaze once again.

"My apologies, sir. The operative who made that mistake won't be making any more. I promise none will be made tracking down what we need right now. I'm heading up to orbit myself once we're done here, and I'm not coming back down until I've got the information we need."

The General Secretary smiled. "Does that mean you're going to remain on board and come along for whatever adventure is next, if you can't solve the riddle before departure?"

"Sir—I appreciate how much you want me to join you and the others who are leaving. Of course, I can't thank you enough for offering me one of our slots. I will once again respectfully decline your invitation."

The Secretary shook his head. "I'm at a loss, Rilee. What's keeping you here? I've shared all of the data with you. You're smart enough to understand what it means for the future of human life on this planet."

She knew the man would never understand, but the answer for Rilee was simple. "This is home, sir. I've spent most of my one hundred and thirty years fighting to save Earth. I realize it's an uphill battle at this point. My family's land sat two hundred kilometers inland when I was born, but the ocean flooded it during this last batch of cyclones. Maybe, just maybe, once the Chancellor has departed along with the rest of her stooges, we'll be able to convince everyone from the West who remains to partner with us and push back the environmental collapse."

"Perhaps someday we'll return to Earth and discover you've accomplished what you seek, Rilee. It's far, far more likely we'll find this planet devoid of human life. Throwing yours away is a tremendous loss for our people, and I have a hard time standing by while you do it. I will respect your wishes, though."

The Secretary tipped his head in a short bow and then spoke again. "What's your plan when you get up to Adan's ship?"

Rilee stood. "I have two operatives embedded in the engineering team you sent who are both equipped with Skins that support remote Upload. One of them has spent the last few months exploring every accessible nook and cranny of the asteroid and has identified high value target areas he thinks we should penetrate. I've held him back to prevent creating any rifts if he was discovered, but it feels like the time for caution is past. On your authority, I will join him and we'll find out whatever we can about what Adan is hiding from us."

The General Secretary nodded. "Make it happen."

"Thank you, sir." Rilee turned and exited the room.

Even after decades of doing her job, the start of a new mission always gave Rilee an electric jolt of excitement. Adrenalin surged through her body as she strode to the small Upload facility within the grounds of the Palace of the Secretariat. She bypassed the handful of lower level bureaucrats queued for processing at the main entrance by walking around the corner to a special check-in desk for senior agents. It was staffed by clerks with the security clearances necessary to be trusted with the comings and goings of the East's top operators. The man behind the desk looked up at her and smiled in recognition. Rilee was a frequent visitor.

"Good morning, ma'am. What's on your Upload agenda today?"

Rilee gave the man an itinerary reference code which he entered into his system. He looked at her again after scanning the details.

"I see you're going up to the asteroid, ma'am. This says you intend to return back to this facility later today. Is that still accurate?"

Rilee nodded.

"Are there any changes you've made to your Pattern while riding this Skin that you want to save? We'll keep it available as long as we can, but I always ask just in case your plans change and we have to return it to feedstock."

Space within the grounds of the Palace was at a premium, so the Upload facility didn't always have enough capacity to keep a Skin warm and available until one's consciousness returned from elsewhere. It was easy enough to generate a new copy from feedstock so most people were indifferent, and Rilee was in and out of Skins so often she rarely gave it a second thought. For once, though, she needed to exert the privilege her rank provided.

"On the General Secretary's authority, my Skin must remain available for immediate Upload when I return. I'm on an urgent mission and won't have any time to wait around for a fresh one to be generated."

"Yes, ma'am. As for the Skin you're targeting up there. This is an acknowledged transfer, correct? Not a forceful takeover?"

"Correct. Please keep his consciousness in a holding pattern for quick return to his Skin once I'm done. I don't want to burn his cover story by leaving the Skin lying around unconscious for too long."

"Yes, ma'am. Please enter room thirty-four. It's almost done calibrating and should be fully prepared by the time you make your way back there. I'll inform the target to expect your imminent arrival."

Rilee nodded at the clerk and then walked past the desk into the warren of Upload rooms that comprised most of the facility. She found thirty-four and entered. Once she stripped naked and folded her clothes neatly, she placed them in a bin so they'd be available for her return. The Upload helmet went on next. She ensured its contact points were adjusted to the proper regions of her scalp, and that it had formed an airtight seal around her neck.

When everything was ready, Rilee keyed a button and the storage tank opened. She attached the umbilical from inside the tank's lid to her helmet and then lay down and allowed herself to achieve neutral buoyancy in the body temperature gel that filled the vessel. The lid closed to seal her in as a countdown flashed on the visor. She closed her eyes and prepared to awaken inside a different body up there on Adan's damned asteroid.

CHAPTER TWO

This is the last piece of the puzzle!

Rilee woke to a stinging sensation and fought against the disorientation that threatened to overwhelm her. Jumping into a new Skin for the first time was an ordeal that could never be totally eased even after years of training and experience. The human brain was astoundingly elastic, but a sense of self was deeply enmeshed in its limbic system and required time and effort to subdue when it was violated by the imposition of a new consciousness. There were techniques that could ameliorate the symptoms, but they could never be extinguished.

She opened her eyes. The Skin had reacted especially poorly to Rilee's arrival and fainted. The coolness of the titanium beneath her seeped through the uniform the Skin wore. A circle of vaguely familiar people in similar uniforms stared down at her prone body. Kadd's was the one face she knew intimately, and he knelt above the Skin with his hand poised to slap its face. Rilee smiled and spoke.

"I'm fine. No need to hit me again."

Kadd stood and extended a hand to help Rilee up off the deck. She clambered to her feet and surveyed her surroundings to establish her bearings. She was in a massive cavern that, based on the craggy appearance of its walls and ceilings, had been hewn out of solid rock. A star field could be seen at one end of the compartment where nothing but an invisible force field separated the hundreds of occupants from the vacuum of space. Her disorientation faded as Rilee recognized she was inside the flight hangar on Adan's asteroid.

As she continued to check out her surroundings, Rilee briefly locked eyes with a familiar adversary. Markev stood sentry ten meters away next to a chair in which the unconscious form of his boss's body reclined. The hulking bodyguard casually appraised the activity of the engineers from the East who had gathered around Rilee's Skin when it collapsed. His face revealed vague curiosity, and she maintained a neutral expression and turned back to Kadd.

"Nothing like announcing my arrival," she whispered.

"Don't worry about it. You won't stand out too much. Lots of people around here have exhibited side effects from the artificial gravity. Something about the system is throwing inner ears off and causing more than a few random falls and fainting spells."

Rilee smiled. Something about the expression was off, and she reached a hand up to discover her mouth was covered by a ragged beard and mustache. Her grin morphed into a grimace.

"I hate facial hair. This Skin wasn't supposed to have any. Why the hell didn't you make sure Joss kept up his grooming standards?"

"Really? You've marooned me on this space rock full of Westerners for the last six months, and you're going to give me grief about someone having a beard?"

Her position in command dictated that Rilee should admonish Kadd for his disrespectful tone, but he had long ago earned the right to call her out when she was being unreasonable. They had become close during fifty years of working together on the front lines of the conflict between the East and West. Their relationship had threatened to get *too* close during one particularly intense mission last year, so it was just as well this time around she was riding a male Skin rather than her personal Pattern. Kadd had once made it clear how he had no interest in the male body, regardless of the gender of the consciousness within. She smiled again instead.

"Fine. You're right. Sitrep?"

Kadd pointed to the hangar's exterior entrance. Its force field had started to slowly flash green. "You're just in time to witness Adan's return from his first flight Uploaded into one of the new fighters." Kadd grabbed Rilee by the elbow and pulled her away from the larger group. He covered his mouth and spoke softly. "Our responsibilities here will be done once Adan's back in his body. Then we can go discuss the two infiltration targets I detailed in my report."

"Sounds good. What's my role on this team? How will I know whatever it is I'm supposed to be doing?"

"Don't worry. When I was informed you'd be joining us, I arranged for Joss to be an observer while I operated the Upload console. Just keep your eyes open and your mouth shut. *Ma'am*."

Rilee appreciated the honorific, but she sure didn't feel like a *ma'am* with the tangle of facial hair causing her to itch. She'd have to be mindful that scratching her face didn't become a compulsion while she rode this Skin. Damned Joss.

A klaxon wailed and Rilee turned to the hangar entrance as a fighter pierced its force field. She had studied the engineering schematics the team from the East had managed to locate and send to Earth, but she hadn't seen images of a completed craft. Its sleek silhouette belied the tremendous power and destructive capacity Rilee knew the fighter possessed. She didn't understand why Adan believed he needed such craft for a simple colonization mission, but he had created a masterpiece of a war machine.

The fighter floated ten meters above the deck, and Rilee was struck by the near silence of its propulsion system. The craft had appeared to be a tiny drone when it was framed by the immense hangar's entrance, but as it approached her position, Rilee got a better sense of its true size. For something twenty meters long to fly indoors while generating barely any discernible noise was tribute to what Adan and his team had built. She didn't like the man one bit, but it was impossible to not admire what he had accomplished.

The fighter gently touched down, and engineers swarmed around it. One of the team members from the East approached the craft trailing a cable that led back to the console Kadd and Rilee stood in front of. The consciousness transfer could have been achieved far more efficiently with their remote Upload process, but the General Secretary had wisely withheld that secret technology from Adan and instead provided him with only their first generation, wired capability.

The tech secured the cable to a port on the fighter and then turned to Kadd with a thumbs up. He triggered the system checks which flashed a series of green symbols once they were done. Kadd called out.

"Markev—everything checks out. We're ready to transfer him back into his body."

The bodyguard gave a thumbs up, and Kadd initiated the transfer process. It took every ounce of willpower for Rilee to not push Kadd away from the controls and initiate the secret control sequence that would sabotage the transfer and shred Adan's consciousness. The East's leadership had debated this alternative extensively, but then concluded it would be far too counterproductive. As much as they despised the man and his efforts on behalf of the West, they wanted their culture to escape Earth and be guaranteed survival out among the stars. Those from the East who were abandoning their homeworld needed a ride into the future, and Adan was the only viable option.

The console signaled completion of the transfer process, and Rilee turned her attention back to the chair. Adan's eyes were open as he stirred. Markev stood next to his boss and gazed down at him. After a few moments, Adan shook his head a couple of times while blinking like he was trying to wake from a nap. His face broke into a grin, and he laughed before speaking loudly enough for his voice to carry to where Rilee stood.

"We've done it, Markev! This is the last piece of the puzzle!"

The burly man nodded as he extended a hand to assist Adan up out of the chair. Rilee turned to Kadd and spoke softly.

"Well, it looks like someone admires the work you've all done. Somehow, I feel a little odd congratulating you. If I live for a thousand years, I still don't think I'll understand what the General Secretary was thinking by sharing our Upload technology with these people. And in Adan's case, especially, I use the word *people* loosely."

Kadd continued his activities on the console and didn't look up as he replied. "I kept waiting for an order to halt progress and destroy everything, but it never came. It's long since moot now. The same way we know enough to replicate their fighter technology on our own, you can bet they've got everything they need to reproduce our Uploading system without our assistance."

Kadd went quiet as he manipulated the screens on the console. Rilee waited for the man to finish, and after a minute he looked up at her.

"We're done here. I'm starving and the mess hall is a reasonable place for us to talk."

Rilee nodded and spun around in the direction where she had earlier noticed an exit. Her mind had not yet established full spatial awareness in the new Skin, so she was oblivious to the fact someone was walking past. The body she slammed into was unyielding like a solid wall and it took all of her training to react nonchalantly when she bounced off Markev. She had been this close to the giant of a man before, but she had been in the comfortable confines of her personal Pattern and he had been lightly sedated and thoroughly restrained.

"Watch where you're going, dammit."

Markev's tone was dismissive, and he didn't look at Rilee as he brushed past. He was following a few paces behind Adan who must have passed by while Rilee had been focused on Kadd's activity. She was prepared to stammer out an apology, but Markev didn't break his stride or slow his pace. She turned to Kadd and found the man chewing his lip in a poor attempt to stifle laughter. He finally barked out a brief chuckle.

"Smooth. Really, really smooth. I've been working here since before breakfast. Let's go get some lunch."

CHAPTER THREE

Sounds like a plan.

K add led as Rilee carried her tray loaded with food. They passed a number of empty seating areas and instead chose a table in the middle of the most crowded portion of the mess hall. Blending in was critical and background noise was much more helpful for hiding quiet conversation than isolation. Rilee allowed Kadd to eat for a few minutes while she did the same. She already had lunch back on Earth, but Joss must not have eaten for quite a while because she was physically famished.

Rilee scratched at the Skin's scraggly facial hair, and a crumb fell to the table. The only thing worse than the constant itching was the prospect of walking around with stray food unknowingly stuck to her face, and the thought made Rilee shiver. She dropped her fork in disgust and stole a glance at the bracelet on the wrist of the Skin. It was camouflaged to appear like a simple piece of jewelry, and Rilee briefly fantasized about pressing the small green jewel that would trigger her Upload and provide an escape to her personal Pattern on Earth. She'd never quit a mission that way, of course, but it was an attractive option to ponder until Kadd slowed the pace of his eating.

"Tell me about what you've been doing up here."

Kadd took a last bite and spoke once he was done chewing.

"Per your orders, I've been cautious with my exploration and haven't taken any high-risk action. I've visited as much of this rock as possible under the guise of running for exercise while carrying different sensors hidden on my body."

Rilee smiled. "I noticed you lost some weight. I had thought maybe the meals up here weren't up to your standards, but after watching you devour lunch that explanation doesn't seem likely."

"The food here is great—by Western standards. Say what you will about Adan, but he's taken good care of the Westerners he's brought up here to build this ship of his. Even though large portions of the asteroid are off-limits without special clearance, I estimate I've been able to log sufficient distance to get within sensor range of eighty to ninety percent of its overall volume."

Kadd paused for another couple of bites and then continued.

"Every night I extracted the sensor data and combined it with everything else I'd gathered to build a virtual model of the ship. We can review it back in my quarters. There are two discoveries that need further investigation. First, I've detected trace radiation emanating from an area of the ship where there isn't any official reason for it to be present."

Rilee nodded. "That explains the equipment you requested."

"Yes. The radiation is coming from a compartment where there's only a single entrance with tight security. My sensor detected its presence, but the radiation is so faint I can't get a more detailed analytical profile to nail down what type of material is present and what purpose it might serve. I haven't been able to come up with any good ideas about how to get a larger sample to test without risking discovery."

"Let's come back to that. Tell me about the other target you've identified."

Kadd was about to continue when he shifted his glance to a spot over Rilee's shoulder. A group was talking loudly as they approached from behind, so she picked at her food and waited for them to pass. Their voices grew louder and louder until Rilee bolted upright from the shock of ice cold water showering down her face.

As the group laughed, Kadd popped out of his seat, hurdled over the table, and tackled the worker from the West who had poured the contents of his cup over Rilee's head. She jumped out of her seat and shouted.

"Don't do it!"

Kadd's arm was already cocked as Rilee's words echoed out. He stopped his fist before it reached the man's face and a moment later was himself thrown to the deck by one of the assailant's companions. Rilee reached over, yanked the third worker into an embrace, and jammed her fork against the soft tissue beneath one of the man's eyes. Rilee pitched the Skin's voice as low and threatening as she could make it.

"You need to walk away right now unless you want to be searching for your friend's eyeball under the table."

The worker who had narrowly avoided getting his face crushed by Kadd glared at Rilee for a moment but then stood up and spoke.

"They're not worth it, guys. Let's get going."

The second man got up off Kadd and the two of them began to walk away. Rilee released her grip on the third and pushed him in his coworkers' direction. He stopped for a moment to scowl at her, but then scampered away to catch up with his friends. The group's laughter was loud enough to carry over the background noise as they left the mess hall.

The scuffle had attracted attention from those nearby, but everyone turned back to their food once it became clear there wouldn't be any entertainment. Rilee ran her fingers through her sodden hair to push it out of her eyes while Kadd dusted himself off and sat back down. He calmly started to eat again while she stared at him in disbelief.

"What the hell was that all about? What did Joss do to those guys?"

"I've never seen them before, and I'm confident Joss never has either. It's just a perfect example of the treatment we've been getting up here. We've asked if we could get the same uniforms as everyone else to better blend in, but Adan has insisted we continue to wear these special ones. Our engineers have complained about the situation since they got up here, so I assumed you knew about it."

"Complained to who?"

"Through their chain of command. I know the General Secretary is aware because we got an edict from him stating how we needed to tolerate whatever crap they throw our way. There's a lot of hatred for the East up here, and I can only conclude it emanates from the top down given the degree to which these incidents occur with nothing done to stop them."

Rilee flashed back to the conversation she had witnessed before coming up to the asteroid. The General Secretary had specifically expressed gratitude to Adan about the way everyone from the East was being treated on the spaceship, and she was infuriated to learn the man knew the truth was much different. She had believed him to be a man of principles after working for him for decades, but it appeared he had pushed those aside once he got in bed with Adan and the Chancellor. She was the first to admit how she was too idealistic at times, but the man's integrity struck Rilee as too high a price to bear even if it meant saving himself and the other members of the East's elite who were abandoning Earth and hitching a ride out into the stars.

"I'm sorry you've had to deal with all of this, Kadd. If I had known, I would've tried to change things. Let's get back to figuring out how Adan is trying to screw us over. Tell me about the second target you've identified."

"Sure thing. One of the other sensors I've carried is an ultra-low frequency, ground-penetrating radar. As I travel the ship, it gathers data which allows me to get a sense of what things look like on the other side of walls and hatches I pass. As you would expect, the lower portion of the ship that was carved out of the asteroid is mostly a warren of small compartments connected by passageways. There are a few exceptions where much larger spaces have been blasted out of the rock. The hangar we just came from is one of these. It's ringed by a series of large storage areas that Adan is filling with his various support craft. One of the adjacent caverns is empty, and we're assuming it will get filled with fighter craft now that his design is almost finalized."

Rilee nodded and Kadd continued.

"There's another series of enormous caverns deeper in the asteroid that I haven't been able to identify a purpose for. They're isolated from the rest of the ship as I've never seen anyone coming or going from them. As huge as this starship is, space is still at a premium. Whatever is being done down there must be consequential to Adan for him to dedicate so much interior volume. The entrances are physically sealed and there's no direct way in."

Rilee agreed with Kadd's assessment regarding the attractiveness of the mystery caverns as a target of interest. She had picked up on a phrase in his last sentence.

"Direct way? Are there indirect ones?"

Kadd smiled. "My sensors have identified a series of maintenance tunnels that are otherwise hidden and not shown on any of the asteroid's schematics. I've located an access point that leads into these tunnels and mapped out a path to the caverns of interest. I don't know what kind of security we might run into along the way which is why I haven't taken action and explored further, but if we're ready to take some risks then I believe we can figure out what's going on in there."

Rilee paused and considered Kadd's words. He took the opportunity to finish off the last few bites on his plate and then pointed at her half-eaten meal and raised an eyebrow in an unspoken request. She pushed the tray towards him, and he continued to eat like he hadn't had food in months. Rilee finally spoke.

"Let's first do what we can to penetrate the caverns, and then we can figure out how to obtain a better sample from where you detected the radiation."

"Sounds like a plan. There's some gear in my cabin that will be useful. On the way there we'll also pass by the compartment with the radiation, so you can get a quick look at its security."

CHAPTER FOUR

What the hell was that stunt all about?

Kadd held out his hand and signaled a stop as they approached a turn in the passageway. He knelt and pretended to adjust the fit of his shoes as he whispered.

"The entrance to the target compartment is around the corner. We shouldn't loiter as we pass, but I wanted to give you the heads up so you could pay extra attention."

Rilee nodded and followed Kadd around the corner. It was yet another in a long line of identical passageways, though with one big difference—it included a hatch where two armed sentries stood guard. They were speaking with each other and ignored Kadd and Rilee as they approached, but a quick glance suggested they were well-trained and should not be engaged with lightly.

As Kadd and Rilee got within ten meters of the hatch, it opened and a woman stepped out. Her uniform identified her as some sort of technician, and she nodded at the sentries as she passed by them into the passageway. The sight of the woman's flowing blonde hair triggered an idea for Rilee, and she started talking to Kadd in a loud voice as she gesticulated wildly.

"And then, the guy reached behind him and grabs a blaster I swear was *this* big. And I can see what he's doing, and I know I need to create a diversion, so I spin like this..."

Kadd watched Rilee raptly as she spoke and acted like he had been listening for a while. She demonstrated the spinning portion of her story just as the technician was passing next to them. Her leg darted between the woman's, and the two collapsed to the deck in a heap. The technician berated Rilee as Kadd helped her up off the ground.

"Watch where you're going, you idiot!"

Rilee bowed her head and stammered, "I'm s-s-sorry."

The woman stormed off in a huff, and Kadd extended his hand to assist Rilee. She waved him off and stood without help.

"I'm fine. Let's get to your quarters."

The look in his eyes suggested that Kadd wanted to inquire about what had just transpired, but the agent was smart enough to recognize the tone of her voice. He led them away at a quickened pace, and a few minutes later they arrived at a hatch that opened as Kadd approached. He stepped aside and gestured for Rilee to enter and then spoke once the hatch sealed behind them.

"What the hell was that stunt all about?"

Rilee didn't say a word but instead pointed at her ears and then all around the room. Kadd answered the unspoken question.

"I sweep the room for surveillance devices every day. I have a motion detector in here that would be signaling me right now if anyone had been inside since I left this morning. No one is listening. So once again, why did you crash into the technician like that?"

Rilee smiled as she raised her hand. A flaxen strand of hair was pinched between her finger and thumb.

"Here's the sample you were after. If that woman was working in the radioactive compartment for any length of time, we'll be able to identify whatever material she was exposed to from her hair. The mass spectrometer we sent you should be plenty sensitive enough to give us a readout."

Kadd's eyes went wide and his mouth broke into a grin that extended from ear to ear. He walked to his closet and lifted a packing case off the deck. He fiddled with it for a moment until a hidden compartment popped open and he pulled something from inside. He returned the case to the deck and then approached Rilee with a hand outstretched.

"My room has been searched often, so I've kept everything important hidden from prying eyes. Let me have that and I'll run it through the spectrometer. It should only take a minute or so."

Rilee handed the hair over. "Thanks. I need to use the toilet while you work."

Kadd stepped aside so Rilee could move past him towards the bathroom. She slid the privacy panel closed behind her and turned to sit as she fumbled with the buckle of the belt Joss had been the one to fasten that morning. Then it hit her.

Different plumbing.

She turned back around to face the toilet. She quit playing with the belt and instead unzipped the pants. Once the Skin's bladder was empty, she zipped up again and washed her hands. Kadd was staring intently at the small screen on the spectrometer when she opened the privacy panel. He looked up as she approached and extended his hand with the device towards her.

"What do you make of this?"

Rilee took the spectrometer and examined its screen. The significance of the analysis struck her and she gasped.

"He's brought offensive nukes up here! I warned the Secretary that Adan would pull a stunt like this, but he didn't want to believe me. Even if he's willing to look past this, there's no way everyone else on the Central Committee will tolerate such a huge treaty violation."

Kadd shook his head. "That's what I was afraid of. Between the fighters we're helping him build and now evidence of nukes, it seems like Adan's trying to transform this asteroid from an ark into a battleship. Why?"

"There's always been rumors the West has evidence of aliens who visited Earth years ago. Maybe those are true, and Adan is assuming they'll encounter more as they seek planets to colonize." Rilee checked the clock before she continued. "I should probably contact the General Secretary with this news, but I know he's in a Committee meeting right now and probably won't answer. Let's go evaluate those caverns of yours. If we find anything else concerning, I can deliver all the bad news at once."

Kadd nodded, walked to his desk, and interacted with the screen of his terminal. After he navigated the system for a few seconds, a holographic image of the asteroid projected into the middle of the compartment. Rilee sat on the bed and leaned back on her arms. A red dot began to flash on the image as Kadd spoke.

"The flashing dot represents our current location." He paused and then a large area towards the bottom of the space rock began to similarly flash. "These are the caverns I've identified. You can see here how gigantic they are which is why I'm so curious about them."

Rilee nodded. "Are you sure it isn't some form of agricultural facility? Something like that could take up that kind of volume."

"You're right about the space requirements for food production, ma'am, but that isn't what this space is for. The agricultural holds are equally huge, but they're open to everyone and I've toured them. These must be something different."

"OK, then. How do we get in?"

"As I stated earlier, all of the visible access hatches are sealed. The caverns are isolated from the rest of the asteroid, so they must be using shuttlecraft to bring people in and out. We could try getting in through those exterior access points, but that strikes me as unlikely to succeed."

Kadd paused and then a dotted line appeared on the image and flashed.

"This line is the path I mentioned earlier through the tunnels I discovered. I've explored the first part and was able to reach a third of the way to the caverns without encountering anyone or getting blocked. We might not make it all the way inside, but I don't know anything else worth trying."

"I agree." Rilee stood up. "Grab the blasters I assume you have hidden somewhere around here. If by some bad luck we run into anyone in those tunnels, we need to keep them silent."

CHAPTER FIVE

Look at your Upload controller.

"This is where I stopped when I first explored these tunnels." Kadd gestured to a ladder that plunged into the depths of a shaft.

Their journey from Kadd's quarters to the maintenance access point and then through the first segment of tunnels had been uneventful. Rilee used the time to focus on mindfulness exercises in an attempt to complete the bond with the Skin she was riding. Using any available downtime to focus on mind-body integration was her favorite technique for shaking off the unavoidable mental disorientation that accompanied Uploading one's consciousness into a new Skin. She gaped down the ladder and shook off a quick blast of vertigo before replying to Kadd.

"Let's do it. You want to lead or follow?"

Kadd grinned. "If you were wearing your Pattern, I'd want to go first so I could steal a glance upwards and admire your ass once in a while. I'd just as soon avoid any risk of that with you riding inside of Joss."

Kadd's dimples were nearly irresistible when he smiled, but Rilee nonetheless regretted again how she had allowed their relationship to pierce the boundary of professional detachment. Her heart yearned to grin back at him, but her brain forced an authoritative grimace and stern words.

"It's no surprise you've never managed to get married if that's your sad idea of flirting. Even sadder given I'm your commanding officer and will beat you senseless if you try it with me again. Get on the ladder."

Kadd's dimples melted away along with his smile. The neutral expression that took their place was betrayed by sadness in his eyes. Rilee regretted the need to be harsh, but she needed him laser focused on their task. He swung his body on to the ladder and, after allowing him a dozen rungs head start, she followed.

They descended level after level, and Rilee found herself grateful that Joss had maintained his physical conditioning even while he allowed his facial grooming to lapse. Even after half a kilometer of nonstop descent, the arms and legs of the Skin did not suffer any ill effects. It might prove otherwise when they climbed out, but Rilee pushed those concerns aside.

Once they reached the bottom of the shaft and she was planted on solid ground, Rilee stretched her legs and back to loosen them. Kadd observed for a moment and then pointed at her left wrist.

"Look at your Upload controller. Same thing with mine."

The jewel on Rilee's bracelet had morphed from green to red. The color signified how the device's connection to the data network was too weak to support an Upload. If there was an emergency, they would be unable to abandon their Skins. Rilee slowly shook her head at the realization the stakes had been raised, and it was now a truly life or death mission. Kadd continued.

"The connection faded in and out a few times on the way down, so I'm hoping they'll lock on to a clean signal again soon."

"Well, let's be extra careful. I'd prefer to not die in this Skin on this rock. Lead the way, please."

Kadd confidently weaved them through a series of tunnels past a number of identical access hatches. Eventually he paused for a moment at one junction and pulled a handful of tiny spheres from his pack. Rilee observed while he pressed a button on each that flipped a light from solid red to flashing. He stuck the miniature orbs in a row along the ceiling of the roughhewn tunnel and then turned to Rilee and handed her a small device the size of her thumb.

"These micro-explosives pack a wallop. If we hit some bad luck and get chased out of here, they'll collapse this tunnel behind us. Flip the cap off this trigger, and then press the button three times in quick succession. I've got a trigger as well in case we get separated."

Rilee grinned in admiration. "Great thinking, Kadd. I've been worrying about how we'd escape if we needed to."

Kadd nodded his appreciation before starting to walk again. Thirty paces later they turned a corner and stopped in front of an access portal. He paused to look at the device in his hand and then addressed Rilee.

"This is our target. On the other side of this hatch is one of the smaller caverns in the mystery complex. I'm hoping that once we get inside we'll be able to find our way into the rest of them. I'm not picking up any signs of life within the fifty-meter range of my sensors, so it should be empty."

"Great work getting us here, Kadd. Let's get inside."

The hatch was different from all the others they had passed. Instead of a simple opening mechanism, it was secured with a biometric reader that controlled access. Kadd pulled out his blaster and aimed at the controller.

"I'll handle this—step back."

Rilee slapped the man's weapon aside. "Put that thing away or you'll get us killed! I've encountered this design before on other infiltration missions. It's alarmed. If you just go at it with brute force, it's going to trigger a failsafe that will keep the door sealed as well as bring all of Adan's guards down on us. Hand me those tools you packed."

Kadd reached into his pack and removed the small toolkit he had brought along. Rilee picked the smallest bladed screwdriver from the kit. From prior experience, she knew the hatch's control mechanism had a flaw where it was possible to work the tip of a tool into position to remove the security cover. A few seconds later it was off and she had exposed the wiring underneath. She traded the screwdriver for a knife and was poised to cut one of the wires when a twinge in her gut gave her pause. Kadd had observed quietly, but when Rilee stopped moving he spoke.

"What's going on? I thought you said you were familiar with this design?"

"I am, and I'm almost positive the gray wire is the correct one to cut. There's something a little different here versus others I've worked on. It's almost like they want us to think it's the same model despite the fact it isn't."

Without another word, Rilee moved the knife from the gray wire to a green one and cut it. She loudly exhaled.

"I guessed right. If that had been the wrong wire, we would've heard security bolts slam shut and seal the hatch. Give me another minute, and I'll have it opened."

Rilee worked to cut and rearrange a half-dozen wires within the console until the hatch cracked open with a loud hiss. She repacked the tools and then handed them back to Kadd. By the time he had them put away in his bag, she had her hand on the hatch and was prepared to open it wider.

"Shall we?"

Kadd took a deep breath and then nodded. Rilee opened the hatch just enough to peek inside. The sliver of visibility revealed a storage area filled with stacks of identical crates. Each was roughly three meters long by one meter high and one meter deep with writing on the side that was illegible from their position. There was no one in sight. Rilee whispered.

"Looks clear. Let's get in there."

She opened the hatch wide enough for them to enter and then pulled it shut behind them. They paused for a moment to listen for any sign of activity. Silence. Rilee pointed towards the closest stack of crates, and they ran there together.

Once they were up close, Rilee examined the text on the crates. They all said the same thing, but it didn't make sense. She turned to Kadd.

"These all contain cryotubes. We know Adan has been lying to everyone about the true passenger capacity of this ship, but I haven't heard anything about putting anyone into cryosleep. Have you?"

"Not a word."

"I don't understand why they'd want to. With the FTL engines, they're going to find planets pretty quickly. Adan has told the Secretary they're expecting to have everyone settled within a dozen years or so."

Rilee didn't expect Kadd to have an answer. She was running through the situation aloud to help process what she was seeing and stimulate her own creative analysis. At that moment, a mechanical rumble filled the cavern. Kadd shrugged in response to her questioning glance.

Rilee peered around the side of the stack they were hidden behind. There was a narrow pathway that led towards where the noise emanated from. She whispered back to Kadd over her shoulder.

"Follow me!"

CHAPTER SIX

What's he going to do with them all?

Rilee darted down the gap. The stacks of crates were separated by a pathway wide enough for two people to move abreast. It was intersected every ten meters with a narrower path that led off at a ninety-degree angle. She could see all the way to where the pile of crates ended.

They ran in a staccato fashion pausing at each intersection to check the cross-path and ensure they were alone. As they reached the end of the stacked crates, the loud rumble halted. Rilee peeked around the stack to the right where there was nothing but empty space. She pivoted her gaze to the left and discovered the source of the noise. An enormous door had slid aside and allowed an automated transport to enter the cavern. It approached a stack of crates with its lift arms extended. Rilee backed up to inform Kadd.

"A transport is pulling a stack of crates out of here. A huge sliding door made all that noise. There aren't any other exits, so if we want to access the other caverns our only chance might be to follow the transport out the main door."

Kadd nodded. "Let's do it."

They turned back toward the edge of the crates and both peered around. The transport had reversed almost all the way out of the storage compartment with a tower of crates perched on its lift arms. A siren wailed three short blasts once the load was clear of the door, and it began to rumble shut again. Kadd tapped Rilee on the shoulder and sprinted toward the shrinking opening. Rilee followed a few paces behind and caught up after Kadd reached the entrance and snuck a glance around the edge. He turned back to her.

"I don't see anyone around. There's cover twenty meters to the left. Follow me."

Kadd bolted around the moving door and Rilee didn't hesitate to follow. She focused on his back as they ran exposed until they reached the spot to hide and survey their surroundings. Rilee's heart pounded from adrenalin as she established her bearings.

Whatever this space was, it was mind-bogglingly huge. Rilee could barely make out the roof of the compartment far above her. They were huddled up against a building of some sort that reached towards the top of the cavern. She estimated it must have been at least three hundred meters tall and two hundred along each side. The exterior material was a smooth, gray titanium that resembled the skin of the various structures built atop the asteroid's surface. The only visible difference from those buildings was that the structure in front of her had zero exterior windows.

Rilee peered around the edge. The cavern extended into the distance as far as she could see. The structure they hid behind was identical to dozens of others that filled the space. The transport they had followed shrank smaller and smaller as it trundled away with its cargo of crates. Rilee's head spun as she tried to decipher what it all meant. She turned back and found Kadd waiting expectantly for an update.

"There's nothing but dozens and dozens of these structures. Let's see if we can find a way inside this one."

Kadd turned and Rilee followed. After fifty meters, they came to a hatch. It wasn't the same design as the other interior hatches within the asteroid but instead resembled an airlock. Kadd checked with Rilee for assent and then activated the hatch. It slid open to reveal a small chamber with another closed hatch at the opposite end. Rilee followed Kadd inside and then he activated the interior hatch. The exterior hatch closed tight before the interior hatch opened. Kadd entered and Rilee followed. She was so shocked by what was inside she stopped in her tracks with her mouth hanging open.

The interior of the structure was a single chamber that appeared to occupy most of its interior volume. It was filled from floor to ceiling with rows and rows of identical capsules—cryostorage tubes. They had been unpacked from their crates and arrayed in stack after towering stack, row after endless row. Kadd spoke.

"I'm confused. If you have this giant cavern and you're going to use it to keep a huge number of people in cryostorage, why create all of these separate structures? Why not just stack them in the compartment?"

"I don't know. Let's see if we can better understand the structure's purpose. This way."

Rilee led them along the exterior wall they had entered through. After a few minutes of walking, they turned a corner and Rilee halted. She turned back to Kadd and pointed up at what she had found. Kadd gasped. It was a sign with arrows pointing in multiple directions. One arrow was labeled with the word *Bridge* and the other had the word *Engineering*.

"There's your answer, Kadd. This isn't a building, it's a transport vessel. Adan has dozens of them. What's he going to do with them all?"

"I'm at a loss, ma'am." He waited for a moment and then asked. "Where should we go first—the bridge or engineering?"

Rilee paused for a moment before answering. "Neither. We know it's a transport of some sort. If I've learned anything, once you've seen one spacecraft bridge you've seen them all. I'd rather figure out how many of these vessels he has."

"Yes, ma'am."

Kadd led them back toward where they had entered the craft. As she followed him, Rilee considered various scenarios about how Adan might be planning to use the vehicles. She kept coming back to one that was most obvious, but too alarming. She needed a count of the vessels to understand just how many people Adan planned to store in order to prove or disprove her theory.

They reached the exit and Rilee followed Kadd through the interior hatch. Once she was inside the airlock, Kadd activated the controls. The interior hatch sealed shut and a second later the exterior hatch opened.

Rilee's head spun and she was moving on auto-pilot as they exited the transport, so the *crack* of a blaster discharge didn't register. What broke her reverie was Kadd falling backward against her. Instinct and training kicked in, and she held him upright against her body rather than let him collapse. A gaping wound had blossomed from the center of his chest and Rilee raised her eyes from it in shock to meet the gaze of the man who had fired the shot.

Markev.

CHAPTER SEVEN

Hand.

Zax cracked open his eyes. It was dark, the lid of his cryotube was still shut, and his cryosuit remained locked in place. After a min of deep breathing he noticed the lights around him were brightening at an almost imperceptible rate that allowed his eyes to adjust without pain.

His mind started to race and his pulse soon followed. How far into the future was he waking? What kind of planet had he been settled on? Would it be a paradise like the last one he had visited, or someplace a lot less hospitable like the first he had ever stepped foot upon? If the Boss was still alive and had any say in the matter, Zax assumed he was part of a colony that had been dumped onto a planet which was one notch above uninhabitable.

The hum of the electromagnets faded, and the lid of his tube opened as his suit was released. Zax sat up. As he did, a voice spoke.

"Get dressed."

Zax clambered out of the cryotube. A drawer in its base slid open and revealed a uniform. Zax stripped out of the cryosuit and was about to don the uniform when his breath was taken away. He was holding the exact same garment he wore the day he was put into cryostorage! There was a small stain on the knee from dinner the night before Zax was Culled, and it still appeared like the food had only been spilled yesterday. There must have been something special about the storage drawer that kept material inside from aging and rotting while the owner slept.

"Follow the arrows."

The door opened and an arrow on the deck outside lit up and pointed to the right. Zax poked his head through the opening and almost leapt for joy. He wasn't on a colony but instead was still on board the Ship! He hadn't been marooned on some horrible planet! His excitement was quickly tempered at the prospect his reprieve might be brief. With his advanced combat training, it was possible he had been woken up to be part of Colonial Security. Perhaps he was only on board for some short training prior to making Landfall.

He followed the arrows through a series of turns until he entered the anteroom of a cryostorage processing facility. It might have been the same one where he had first entered cryosleep, but he assumed they all were the same so it was impossible to know for certain.

The clerk was not the same one who had first processed Zax, but he exuded the same bored indifference. The man extended his arm toward Zax and spoke.

"Hand."

Zax presented his right hand to the man who grabbed it by the wrist. The clerk's other hand came off the workstation and applied a DNA sampler. Zax flinched at the sting as it pierced his finger. He then stared at the screen along with the clerk until it flashed green and showed his name. The clerk turned back to him.

"Your Plug has not yet been reconnected to the Ship. Until that happens, it will function but with limited capabilities. You have fifty-five mins to report to the primary meeting room at the Pilot Academy for a briefing with the Commander, Air Group."

"Fifty-five mins—great. I'm going to stop for some food on the way. I don't think I've ever felt this hungry before in my life."

The clerk shook his head. "The Tube in this region of the Ship is not operational. You'll need all of that time to reach the Pilot Academy. In fact, you might wind up late if you don't double-time it out of here."

There were so many other questions Zax wanted to ask, but the clerk's tone made it clear the man wasn't interested in further conversation. He exited the cryostorage facility and entered an unknown future of the Ship without knowing anything other than his destination.

Zax's primary goal as he walked to the Pilot Academy was to find out how long it had been since he had been put into cryostorage. Was the Ship still on its way towards Earth, or had that destination proven to be a dead end and was long in the past? He planned to put the question to the first person he encountered, but as Zax walked through the Ship he was shocked to not come across a single member of the Crew. His desperation for information was serious enough he considered asking one of the many civilians he encountered, but they were all heavily armed and traveling in large groups. He kept his mouth shut rather than draw attention to himself.

Seeing packs of armed civilians was a significant source of disorientation for Zax, but even worse was the physical condition of the Ship as he moved through its passageways. Every corner he turned revealed greater and greater levels of degradation. Trash was visible everywhere, often in large volumes, and hordes of rodents frolicked among the most festering piles. Zax had become accustomed to stumbling upon an occasional rat as he journeyed through the Ship's hidden maintenance tunnels in the past, but never in his life had he encountered any in the main passageways.

Rubbish and vermin were superficial, but more distressing was the degree to which the Ship's physical systems appeared to be collapsing. Throughout the course of his journey, Zax encountered multiple pools of standing water, large stretches of passageway where primary lighting had failed, and a spot where a tangle of electrical cable had fallen from the overhead and hung at eye level with sparks arcing between the wires.

The most shocking sight of all during his walk was the condition of the Tube. When the clerk mentioned the system was not functioning, Zax had assumed there was a temporary disruption. What he discovered instead was that all of the Tube junctions he passed were torn apart. Given the volume of trash and discarded equipment that surrounded many of them, it appeared that any repair efforts had been long abandoned. The Tube was such a critical service for the Ship that if it had reached such a serious state of disrepair, Zax assumed the overall situation must be dire.

As Zax got closer and closer to the Pilot Academy, he was pleasantly surprised to discover improved conditions. By the time he found the meeting room, the surroundings appeared to be the same as they were the last time he had walked the passageways. He entered the compartment to find it crowded but oddly silent. Usually when Crew gathered for a meeting, they would sit with friends or other people they knew and chat while they waited. Zax found instead a compartment that was full of a cross-section of ages, but where everyone glanced around nervously as if they did not know anyone else. Zax found an empty seat towards the back of the room and waited in silence.

After a few mins the hatch opened and two Crew entered and walked toward the lectern. The woman was facing away from Zax and talking to her male companion, so Zax could only see a small portion of her face. As best as he could tell she was around thirty years old. Her uniform bore the patch signifying she was a pilot along with a second patch with the letters CAG. The Commander, Air Group turned to the group and grinned.

Zax's heart instantly melted. The smile was one which lit up the room in a fashion he was long familiar with. Kalare had become CAG while he was in cryosleep.

CHAPTER EIGHT

Are there any questions?

"Greetings. I imagine all of you are feeling pretty disoriented since you just came out of cryosleep. Unless you were only Culled within the last year or two, you've returned to a Ship you won't recognize. I'm here to help you gain a quick understanding of our situation and the role you have to play now that you've returned to consciousness."

Kalare's voice had deepened and mellowed over the years. Her face had softened as her cheeks filled out. Her hair was longer than he remembered but had somehow become a darker shade of jet-black. He couldn't believe his good fortune that she was standing in front of him as he had entered cryosleep resigned to never seeing her again.

"My name is Kalare, and I became CAG two years ago after my predecessor died in battle. Our foes in that battle, as has been the case in almost every engagement I've ever fought in, were human."

The room was filled with audible gasps. Kalare raised her hands to signal for silence.

"I realize the existence of other humans traveling the stars is shocking information for most of you. We'll make all of our recent history available to each of you once you're Plugged In again so you can understand what has transpired since whenever you were last awake. In the meantime, I'll provide a quick overview.

"We didn't realize it at the time, but we first encountered an unknown group of humans fourteen years ago. Two years later the Ship set a course to return to Earth with our goal being to find those humans. If they were coming from Earth, then perhaps the planet had been saved and we could return there rather than continue our Mission. Within a few months of starting that journey, we encountered the other humans again and were dismayed when they opened fire upon us. We didn't realize they were humans until we found evidence within battle wreckage that confirmed this fact.

"We don't know why they are attacking us because the other humans have never responded to any of our repeated contact attempts. Instead, whenever we encounter them they engage. We've decisively won many of these battles but have had to strategically retreat rather than face defeat in others."

Zax's head spun at the realization the Ship had continued to encounter and battle humans in the years since he had been Culled. He had always assumed that after a few engagements the two sides would realize they were the same species, open lines of communication, and figure out how to coexist. Kalare continued.

"There are two critical pieces of good news to share. The first is that these humans have technology that is very similar to ours. Though they've been lucky during a few battles, we have generally defeated them whenever we've engaged. The other piece of good news is that we've started to encounter the humans far less often over the past year than we have previously. In fact, it has been nine months since we last encountered them. This may mean that they've decided we're no longer worth fighting given how soundly we've defeated them.

"We're entering the final stage of our journey and that's why your group, along with many others like it, have been brought out of cryostorage over the past few weeks. In three months' time, we'll reach Earth. When we do, we want to be prepared for any possible encounter with the other humans. The planet is most likely dead and empty, but if by chance it isn't and we've been battling its inhabitants all along, then we'll be prepared to reclaim it by force.

"Each of you completed your Pilot Academy training or were so close you were practically done. You will spend the next three months drilling and learning the battle tactics we've established over the course of many engagements with the humans. We've harvested asteroids as often as needed and our manufacturing facilities have produced new fighters nonstop. If we encounter the other humans when we reach Earth, we'll be prepared to destroy them with an overwhelming force. Are there any questions?"

A few hands shot up around the room, and Zax raised his as well. Kalare called first on an older female pilot who sat in the front row.

"Ma'am—what makes you think we won't be walking right into a trap of some massive force arrayed around Earth?"

"Good question. For one thing, despite the fact we've encountered the other humans repeatedly across the universe, it appears all of the engagements have been with the same mothership. This is based on its distinctive markings and visible damage patterns. If they had an overwhelming force available to throw at us, we would have dealt with far more than just the same vessel.

"More importantly, we'll be extra cautious as we approach Earth. We'll send scouts ahead and if there is *any* evidence of an advanced civilization and extensive preparations for defense of the planet, then we'll reevaluate our plan."

Kalare called on a male pilot who appeared to be in his mid-twenties.

"Ma'am—as I walked over here I saw dozens of civilians walking around with blasters. When did we start letting civilians carry weapons, and who thought that was a good idea?"

"I can appreciate your curiosity on matters related to the Ship's history since you were Culled. Since some of you were removed from the Crew as far back as two thousand years ago, there's just too much information that would be necessary to reorient all of you. I'll ask that you please wait until we can point you to resources where you can gain that historical context yourself. In the meantime, I'm happy to answer any questions related to our current situation."

The other cadets lowered their hands, and Zax was the only person remaining with his raised. Kalare glanced at him as she scanned the room, but she didn't acknowledge him and spoke to the group instead.

"Since there aren't any other questions, you're dismissed until tomorrow. There are terminals behind me that will direct you to the berth you've been assigned. Go get some sleep and report to the training facility at 0900 tomorrow."

Zax's spirits crashed at the realization Kalare had intentionally avoided him. He sprang from his seat in an attempt to reach her, but she turned and left while Zax got tangled in the crowd of Crew making their way to the front of the compartment. By the time he weaved his way down to the hatch, she had disappeared. Zax pounded his fist against the bulkhead and then stomped back into the compartment to check for his berth assignment.

CHAPTER NINE

There can't be any middle ground.

Kalare managed to walk through the hatch but then broke into a sprint once she knew she was out of sight of the meeting room's occupants. She needed to escape before Zax had any chance to catch up with her. Despite her confidence about seeing him again, her heart had threatened to beat its way out of her chest throughout the briefing.

Twelve years! It might as well have been twelve lifetimes ago that she had pounded on the glass and screamed as her best friend was led into the cryostorage facility. Kalare had gotten older, of course, but Zax hadn't aged a day. The emotions dredged up by the memories were almost too much for her to tolerate.

She ran from cryostorage processing that morning long ago and tracked the Boss down in a staff meeting. Kalare had barged in and started screaming nonsensically. The Boss dismissed his staff and then calmly asked her what was wrong. When Kalare was composed enough to be coherent, she told him about Zax and the Boss appeared shocked. He asked her to wait while he closed his eyes and made some inquiries via his Plug. After an eternity, he opened them and fixed her with a look of grave sorrow.

There's nothing I can do. This can't be changed. I'm sorry.

She begged for more details, but the Boss stressed it was a matter restricted to Omega knowledge only and reiterated there was no way he could change the outcome.

Kalare had stormed away to speak with that weird friend of Zax's, Mase, but that proved fruitless as well. The boy listened at first, but then he got up and walked away without another word as soon as she told him what the Boss had said when asked what he knew about the Culling. From that point onwards, every time she approached him the boy would get away from her as fast as possible.

Even though the memories of Zax never faded completely, the pain associated with his Culling waned with time. Kalare's healing was no doubt helped by the degree to which she threw her energies into her work as a pilot. She quickly rose through the ranks until she became the youngest person in almost a thousand years to earn the title of CAG. Kalare understood the Boss had likely exerted some influence behind-the-scenes to make it all happen, but he never said anything and she never asked.

A light flashed in her field of vision to signify an incoming connection via her Plug.

"*Good evening, Boss. What can I do for you?*"

"*Hello, Kalare. I think you know what I'm pinging you about.*"

"*Of course, sir. I appreciate you checking in on me. Everything went fine with Zax. We didn't get a chance to speak, but I'll be sure to connect with him in the next couple of days once he's had a chance to get reacclimated.*"

The Boss paused. Kalare knew that if they were face-to-face the man would be fixing her with one of his penetrating gazes. He'd stare until he identified the most subtle body language that would contradict her words.

"*OK, Kalare. I appreciate how calm you're being about all of this, but I don't believe you're handling it as well as you want me to think. I can't imagine the mix of emotions his return must bring up for you, but I need you focused on making him a productive contributor again. He was such an amazing pilot and probably the only one who might have beaten you out for CAG if he had chosen a different path. Thank you for being such a consummate professional.*"

The Boss cut the connection before Kalare could reply. She was grateful because it prevented her from making an observation about the man's choice of words. *If he had chosen a different path.* The phrase could be interpreted a number of different ways where Zax and the Boss were concerned, and it was probably best she didn't have a chance to probe. The fractious relationship between her friend and her mentor had caused repeated friction between the Boss and Kalare in the past, and she didn't need to invite any of that drama back into their lives given the challenge the Ship was gearing up for.

What would they find when they reached Earth? Kalare's honest hope was it would be long dead and the Ship would resume its Mission out among the uncharted universe. They hadn't encountered the other humans for the longest period in years, so perhaps they might never see them again if they kept traveling away from where their encounters had been frequent.

The absolute worst thing, from Kalare's perspective, was any notion they would take the planet by force if they found Earth inhabited by the humans they had battled for years. Kalare was willing to kill in defense of the Ship, but she had a hard time justifying a decision to violently evict members of their own species from their shared ancestral homeworld. After all, Kalare's ancestors had voluntarily left the planet five thousand years ago. If someone else had managed to save Earth, it only seemed proper to Kalare they should keep it. She had tried to argue the point with the Boss on more than one occasion, but the man never took the bait. He always shut her protestations down by saying he had no choice but to follow the President's orders.

Kalare reached her quarters and paused at the hatch before entering. She took a few deep breaths to purge the last of her stress, only to have it spike again when she tripped over a red uniform on the deck right inside the hatch. Even years later, she still wasn't quite used to the idea of sharing her personal space with someone else. She appreciated romantic companionship and all it entailed, but she hadn't quite figured out how to reconcile the fact that two people could have such wildly different definitions of what *neat and tidy* meant. She called out.

"Haven't I asked you a million times to not leave your uniforms on the deck? It's bad enough you usually reek of Engineering, and the funk in here only gets worse when you leave dirty clothes laying around."

Silence. She called again.

"Hey—are you here?"

Kalare smiled when her words were met again with silence. Unexpected time to herself was a nice way to end a tough evening. She chose to wash the rest of her tension away with a long, hot shower. Rank came with privileges, and being CAG afforded one of the most amazing and sought-after benefits on the Ship— private bathing facilities in her suite. She pushed open the door to her sleeping area with her butt as she wrestled her uniform shirt up over her head.

Before she could process what was happening, Kalare's body was lifted off the deck and slammed on to her bed. An instant later, she was held down with knees on either side of her chest and her hands pinned down over her head with her arms entangled in the shirt.

"Dammit, Aleron! Let me get my shirt off—I can't breathe!"

Once her hands were released, Kalare wriggled out of her shirt and grinned up at Aleron. He must have just stepped out of the shower as damp hair was stuck to the side of his face. She playfully pushed him off, and he rolled over and lay sideways facing her.

"How are you? How did things go with Zax?"

Kalare's cheeks started to flush, but she didn't break eye contact. "Fine."

Aleron paused and appraised Kalare's expression before replying with a hard edge to his voice. "You didn't tell him about us."

"Look, Aleron, I didn't talk to him at all, OK? I'll get around to it when I can, but we're gearing up for a potential major battle here. It's not like I would try to hide anything from him. Why would I at this point? He's practically still a boy, remember?"

"It's not that simple, Kalare, and you know that. In Zax's mind, it was just yesterday you two were best friends, and I was the idiot who had bullied him his entire life. You've had twelve years to move on with your life. It's going to be impossible for him to catch up with that head start any time soon, but you've got to help him begin the process with an honest conversation. Or you've got to stay away from him entirely. There can't be any middle ground."

"Thanks, but if I need any tutoring about emotions from you, I'll be sure to ask for it explicitly. In the meantime, please keep your opinions to yourself. I need a shower."

Kalare stomped into the bathing area and flung the privacy divider shut. She blasted the shower as hot as it would go and stepped inside. She bit her lip against the pain until her skin adapted to the temperature. Aleron was right, but Kalare didn't know how she could begin to have that conversation with poor Zax. She owed it to their long-lost friendship to try, and Kalare sobbed silently as the water cascaded over her body and she despaired of the situation.

CHAPTER TEN

Where have you been?

Zax woke after a fitful night's rest. He had lived his entire life sharing a berth with four hundred cadets, so he had never developed any expectation of privacy. That was very different from his new living quarters, however. The massive space where Zax had trained on battle simulations with the Marines years earlier had been converted into temporary quarters for all of the pilots pulled out of cryostorage. It held enough bunks, stacked ten high, for ten thousand people. There were still a few empty rows, but it was close to being full.

Whoever managed the huge berth had pumped in white noise, and Zax was grateful he didn't have to listen to thousands of people snoring all night long. Just knowing there was such a massive crush of humanity in his immediate vicinity made real sleep impossible, though, regardless of the aural distraction. That and the fact his stomach grumbled something fierce all night long. The mess hall was no longer open around the clock, so there hadn't been any food available by the time the previous night's briefing had ended.

Zax climbed down from his berth halfway up the stack and followed signs to a bathing facility. As he entered he caught the eye of an older pilot who walked out visibly shivering. She grimaced as she spoke.

"Cold water again today, dammit. They keep saying we'll have hot water soon, and then nothing comes of it. There are seriously days I've wondered if I would've been better off waking up on a colony instead."

Without another word, the woman brushed past Zax towards the sleeping quarters. He paused for a moment to consider his options. There hadn't been any mention of a Leaderboard, so he assumed there wouldn't be any consequences for skipping a shower. Even so, all of his old conditioning nagged that he would be remiss to not wash twelve years of cryostorage off his body before heading to breakfast. He stripped and forced himself to scrub for almost three full mins under the icy stream.

Once Zax was dried and dressed, he made his way towards the mess hall. He battled a sense of disorientation with every step. Even though conditions were better around the Crew areas, he couldn't shake memories of the overall dysfunction and disorder he had witnessed so graphically on the walk yesterday. There wasn't as much visibly broken equipment, but there was still far, far more than he ever remembered seeing years earlier.

Worse than the changes in the physical environment of the Ship were the changes in the emotional atmosphere that surrounded Zax. As much as life in the Crew had always been high stress, there was still a sense of purpose from everyone being aligned around the fight to reach the top of the Leaderboard. Twelve years later, Zax had been dropped into a huge pool of Crew rejects who had all suffered the indignity of the Cull. He assumed they would be provided more motivation than being asked to blindly defend a culture that had previously cast them off, but that remained to be seen.

All of that paled, of course, to the ultimate indignity of having his best friend literally turn her back on him. There was no doubt she had seen him, and yet she ignored his raised hand and then fled the compartment before he could catch up to her. Even as bad as things were on the Ship, Zax remained grateful about his return. He couldn't imagine ever agreeing with the woman from earlier about how it might have been better to wake up on a colony instead.

He entered the mess and was struck by how many civilians were present. Whereas in the past they might have occupied a handful of tables, they now filled more than half the compartment. Zax approached the sweets station and noticed his favorite breakfast pastry was missing. He flagged down a staffer.

"I'm looking for those flaky pastries with the sweet fruit filling. Do you have any more?"

The young man stared at Zax for a moment and then started to laugh. "Where have you been? We haven't had any of those for years." He continued to shake his head and cackle as he walked away.

Zax, shoulders slumped, loaded up his tray and shuffled into the seating area. He was about to give up on finding a table where he could sit by himself when he noticed a group standing to leave near the spot where he and Kalare used to have so many of their morning discussions. It was three civilians, and Zax's mouth hung open in shock when they walked away and abandoned their dirty dishes and trash on the table. He stared after them for a moment in disbelief before pushing one of the trays off to the side to clear space for his own. The morning newsvid began to blare around the room just as Zax tore greedily into his first meal in years.

"We start this morning with hearty congratulations to the many fine civilians in our Maintenance unit who keep the Ship in such a great state of cleanliness and operational readiness. They have met or exceeded their success metrics for the past three hundred days, and the President felt it was time they received some well-deserved recognition for the accomplishment."

Zax almost choked on the toast he was swallowing. From his experience, over less than a day awake, he couldn't begin to comprehend what kind of metrics President Imair might have set for the Maintenance team if they were being publicly lauded for exceeding them. If the current state of the Ship was grounds for celebration, Imair had dramatically adjusted her viewpoints about what constituted acceptable performance from when Zax had worked with her in Waste Systems. The announcer continued.

"On a somewhat more sober note, we have news that one thousand civilians were put out an airlock last night as a result of their participation in the destructive riot we reported on two days ago. Here's the President to explain more about the justification behind their punishment."

Zax was so astonished by what was on the screen that he sent a mouthful of half-chewed food across the table. His vision narrowed to a tunnel, and the tumult around him in the mess hall disappeared as if he had been struck deaf. No noise registered for Zax even as the President's lips moved on the screen.

Rege's lips.

The man had aged poorly, but there was no doubt it was the greasy civilian's face that stared back out of the vid. Zax's head spun as he tried to process what he was seeing when a sound cut through his shock. It was someone repeating his name.

"Zax? Is it really you, Zax?"

It was a voice he didn't recognize. A bass that was far too deep to emanate from the face of the young stranger who peered down at Zax. The speaker was tall—well over two meters—with muscular arms and a broad chest that stretched his uniform taut. His hair was dirty blond and worn somewhat longer than regulation. Recognition finally struck Zax.

"Mase!"

CHAPTER ELEVEN

It's making me crazy!

The man who young Mase had transformed into, spoke.

"I was on the other side of the room and you caught my eye. I couldn't believe it was you. Then I walked up and saw the way you were focused on the newsvid. I've seen that look of shocked disbelief before. It's great to see you, Zax."

"Wow, Mase, I barely recognize you. The last time we were together you barely came up to my shoulders, and now you're towering over me."

The man grinned as he sat down. "I had a growth spurt when I was eighteen. You look exactly the same." Mase shifted uncomfortably. "I'm sorry. That was a stupid thing to say."

Zax waved off the comment. "Don't worry about it. That's the absolute least of my worries. You're not the only unrecognizable thing around here. Why does everything seem like it's about to collapse? How did Rege become President?"

Mase looked around and then hunched his frame down to be closer to Zax while he spoke softly. "Haven't you been told what has happened since you went into cryostorage?"

Zax shook his head. "Nope. My Plug hasn't been reactivated yet either, so I'm mostly in the dark. Other than hearing about how it's now public knowledge we've been under attack from some other group of humans."

"I guess we've got catching up to do." Mase closed his eyes for a few moments. "I found someone to cover the first part of my training class. I've got a few extra mins to get us started. We'll save the really interesting stuff for when we have more time."

Mase checked their immediate surroundings once again and then dove into his story.

"I was terrified every time a Marine showed up after you got Culled. You said you had kept my involvement secret, but I was still nervous. So, I kept my head down. I focused on the Pilot Academy and halted all of my Artificial Intelligence hacking.

"Your girlfriend tried to get information out of me a few times. I had zero interest in trusting her because of how close she was to the Boss. I didn't want her getting me in trouble with him given he was the one who took you down."

Zax grimaced at the mention of Kalare and her relationship with the Flight Boss, but Mase either missed or ignored it and kept talking.

"I graduated from the Pilot Academy as Maverick since you were gone. They assigned me to Blue Squadron. I was flying a combat air patrol when we had our next interaction with the humans a few months later.

"We were about to start a refueling operation when they jumped into the system. They shot at us straight away. I recognized the craft and assumed the Boss would say something. Or anyone else who had seen the video you took of that first fighter you found. No one ever did.

"This pattern continued until we disabled one of their craft in a battle instead of shattering it. We took it apart and discovered it contained a biological matrix for holding an uploaded consciousness just like our fighters—a matrix built from human DNA!"

Zax appreciated how Mase wanted to give him the full history, but he found himself growing impatient. Having just emerged from the punishment for his earlier conflict with the Boss, the fear of getting dragged back into any conspiracy-mongering weighed heavily on Zax. Mase continued.

"When it was clear we were fighting humans we started talking about what would happen when we reached Earth. The Omegas seemed nervous about whether we'd defeat the others with our standard complement of fighters. They announced a plan to construct an overwhelming force that also meant thawing out enough pilots to help retake the planet by violence if necessary.

"Right around that time the Ship's condition took a nosedive. People kept blaming it on how we were directing so many of our resources into building the extra fighters. That excuse never made a lot of sense to me. The civilians who do maintenance are different from those involved in fighter production."

Zax's patience was exhausted, so he interrupted when Mase paused for a breath.

"Can you please jump to what happened to Imair and how Rege became President? I keep seeing his face on the newsvid playing behind you. It's making me crazy!"

"Sorry, Zax. I should have known how interested you'd be about him after the stories you shared with me. In my defense, that was twelve years ago."

Mase grinned once again, and Zax returned the expression with a wan smile of his own. He wasn't nearly as quirky as he had been when they first met, but Mase still struck Zax as being quite odd. He continued.

"You might remember there had been increasing amounts of violence in the civilian sector when you were still awake. Shortly after you were Culled there was a massive riot. It went on for weeks until Imair gave in to their demands and stepped down in favor of Rege. She hasn't been seen or heard from since. I'm guessing she got tossed out an airlock. I've looked but haven't been able to uncover any confirmation about that."

Mase's last sentence caught Zax's attention. "I thought you stopped poking around in the AI systems?"

"Well, I did for a while after you got Culled. Eventually I got bored with my regular duties and started digging around in there again. I'm actually on the verge of cracking something I think might be incredible. I don't have enough time to explain it all to you now. If I've found what I think I have it's going to be huge news."

Mase looked at Zax excitedly as if he expected to be pushed for more details about his cryptic comments. Zax was too busy thinking about what Rege being in charge might mean for him to care much about whatever Mase was hinting at. He stood instead.

"Thanks for the information, Mase. It's good to see you. I really need to be leaving now or else I might be late for my first training class."

"It's good to see you too, Zax. We should start eating together again. For old times' sake."

Zax smiled and turned to leave. *Old times indeed.*

CHAPTER TWELVE

That was a warning shot.

Rilee didn't hesitate. She ducked her head behind Kadd and dragged him backwards as a shield. His body jerked from additional blaster impacts as she scurried towards the interior hatch. She triggered the control mechanism and breathed a momentary sigh of relief as the exterior hatch slammed shut with Markev and his blaster on the other side. She heaved Kadd through the interior hatch once it opened and then sealed it behind them. Rilee drew her blaster and fried the airlock control panel in an attempt to prevent immediate pursuit.

She gently laid Kadd on the ground and clutched for a pulse at his neck. The Upload controller on his wrist still shone red, but it was moot for the agent. His Skin was dead and his consciousness was irretrievably gone along with it. Tears welled, but Rilee blinked to fight them off. It was rare to witness permanent death, and she was momentarily overwhelmed. She choked her feelings down since she knew there was no time to mourn Kadd's death if she wanted to avoid her own.

The information Rilee possessed was critical for the General Secretary, and she had to get to a location where her controller could establish a clean connection for Upload. Her best idea was to move higher within the transport. If they had lost the connection as they descended the ladder, perhaps gaining altitude would get away from whatever interference was blocking the signal. The sign from earlier popped back into her mind and she bolted in the direction it had pointed for the bridge. She desperately hoped this spacecraft's main control center was like most others and located at a high vantage point on its structure.

Rilee rejoiced at discovering a lift, but her excitement evaporated when an explosion echoed through the transport and signaled her head start on Markev would be far less than hoped. He had simply blown his way through the disabled airlock. The lift door shut and thirty seconds later Rilee exited onto a level that must have been perched atop the structure. A sign pointed down a corridor towards the bridge. Her controller had acquired a marginally stronger signal, but Upload was still blocked.

Rilee sprinted until a plasma bolt tore her blaster out of her hand as she entered a junction where two corridors crossed each other. She spun back the way she had come, pressed herself against the bulkhead for cover, and cursed whatever bad luck had allowed Markev to find her so fast. The man's voice boomed out.

"That was a warning shot. If I wanted you dead, you would be. There's no sense running because I stuck a tracker on you when I bumped against you back in the hangar. Save us all this worthless drama and give yourself up, or next time it might be a kill shot."

Rilee didn't want to give up without a fight, but her options were woefully limited. Then, an almost imperceptible *click* offered hope. Markev was swapping out the energy clip on his blaster. Rilee recognized her chance and bolted from behind her cover to sprint across the gap.

Four meters.

Three meters.

She glanced to her left where Markev sheltered behind a corner, fifty meters down the intersecting corridor while he slammed a fresh energy clip into his weapon.

Two meters.

One meter.

Rilee dove for cover as shots echoed next to her. The acrid smell of cooked flesh revealed that she had not made it safely into the clear as she rolled out of the corridor junction. When she tried to stop her roll with her left arm, she instead fell flat on her face. Her left hand had been replaced by a cauterized stump midway below her elbow, and its absence caused her to over-rotate and lose balance. The beginnings of agony threatened to overwhelm the nerve blocks in her Skin when the fresh wound slammed into the deck.

Far, far worse than any pain was discovering her Upload controller bracelet was still attached to the wrist of the severed hand that lay smoldering behind her. Charging footsteps echoed as Markev gave chase. Rilee could abandon the controller, but that would mean riding this Skin to her capture or death.

She jumped to her feet and ran back towards the corridor intersection. Rilee made her footfalls as heavy as possible to attract Markev's attention. At the last possible moment, she dropped to the deck and slid on her backside. Plasma bolts passed overhead at a height which would have been center mass had she stayed upright.

Rilee snatched her left hand from the deck with her right as she slid past by intertwining the fingers of both. Despite the severed hand losing blood flow only a few moments earlier, the temperature difference between the two hands had become noticeable. Rilee pushed up off the ground and used her momentum to pull her legs back under her and continue her sprint. She exited the corridor junction just as a new round of plasma impacted the space where her head had been a moment ago.

Left turn.
Right turn.
Left turn.
Left turn.

Rilee barreled ahead as fast as she could to put distance between her and Markev. Her eyes registered a flash of the color green and she glanced down to discover her controller had acquired a signal. It was weak and barely acceptable, but it was sufficient for Upload. She ducked into the next compartment she passed and found herself in a supply closet. It was an obvious hiding spot and even more useless if Markev had indeed affixed her with a tracker, but Rilee only needed a few moments to render the chase moot.

She wedged the door shut with her back by bracing her feet against the opposite bulkhead, and then Rilee slipped the dead hand under her armpit so she could manipulate the controller on its severed wrist. She pressed the green jewel on the bracelet and closed her eyes in anticipation of Upload.

Nothing.

She jabbed at the jewel a second time but again nothing happened. Then cold realization dawned. Of course the controller was having zero effect—it was grafted onto the nerves of her wrist, and with the hand severed, there was no way for its electrochemical signals to trigger Upload. It should have been obvious from the start, and she could only blame the physical shock to the Skin for why it hadn't registered sooner.

The supply closet door bowed inwards as Markev attempted to force it open. One, two, three times he charged, and each time Rilee kept the door closed with her legs braced against the opposite bulkhead. After a brief pause, his blaster started up again, and plasma rounds hammered the door. The countdown to her death was on. The door was lightly armored but would not hold up for long against a weapon at point blank range.

Rilee had only one chance at escape. She reached over to the stump of the dead hand tucked under her arm and tried to scratch at it with her right hand. Joss had kept his nails trimmed short, and they found no purchase on the leathery toughness of the cauterized wound. The plasma had sheared off the hand and sealed the stump tight. She was indenting the giant scab, but not enough to make a difference. She grimaced at the realization of what she needed to try next and lifted the hand to her mouth.

She gingerly brought her jaws together and gently gnawed at the wound. The scab had the texture of an old shoe, and Rilee forced herself to clench her teeth tighter and tighter in an effort to puncture it. Finally, Rilee gagged as coppery blood oozed into her throat. She pried the wound open with her two front teeth and peeled off two-thirds of the burnt tissue at the end of the wrist stump.

"So much for the easy part," Rilee muttered as she turned her attention to the cauterized end of her arm and brought the stump up to her mouth. Unlike the severed hand, the wound that terminated Rilee's limb was filled with nerve endings that were still connected to her brain. All Skins were configured to modulate nerve activity and not overwhelm the rider with negative inputs, but there was only so much pain that could be effectively blocked. The first chomp of Rilee's teeth buckled her knees and grayed her vision.

As she fought to retain her senses, the door at Rilee's back became uncomfortably warm. The incessant blaster rounds were about to breech it. With newfound desperation, Rilee worked at the edge of the giant scab until her teeth punctured it. Unlike the lukewarm ooze of blood that came from the detached hand, removing a portion of the scab on her arm resulted in a geyser of hot blood that pulsed in time with Rilee's quickened heart.

The only thing that prevented her from blacking out from the shock was a new burst of white-hot pain that consumed Rilee's consciousness. A gaping exit wound had blossomed from her belly as the blaster working to puncture the door completed its mission. Rilee's legs wobbled and then gave out as she slid to the deck. With all the will she could summon with the Skin's final breath, Rilee swung her right arm towards her left and brought the bloodied stumps of her arm and the severed hand together at the same moment she pressed the green jewel on the controller.

Everything faded to black with Rilee's panicked realization that her Upload had triggered but something was terribly wrong.

CHAPTER THIRTEEN

He did what?

Rilee woke with a start and recoiled at the brightness. She clenched her eyes shut and then only cracked them gradually wider as they adjusted to the light and she could take in her surroundings. The room was windowless and featureless. It was either part of a medical clinic or perhaps a detention facility. The latter only entered her mind when she attempted to lift her arms and discovered they were held down by restraints. Her answer came a moment later when the door opened and a woman entered in medical scrubs. Rilee was flooded with a sense of déjà vu as the woman spoke.

"Greetings. I'm glad to see you're awake again."

"Again? This is the first time I've seen this place."

The woman looked at her with a mix of pity and benevolence. "This is the first time you *remember* seeing this place. You've been awake for short stints a couple of dozen times. The first few you went into a violent rage and attacked staff which is why you're in the restraints. You've been getting progressively more lucid."

That explained Rilee's sense of having lived through this scene before. "Where am I?"

The medic sat on the edge of the bed next to Rilee's leg. "You're back on Earth. This clinic is part of the Palace of the Secretariat. The General Secretary insisted we keep you here so he could verify himself that you were getting the best possible care."

"Care...what's wrong with me?"

"We're not sure what happened. Our best guess is there was an interference spike of some sort when you were Uploading. It scrambled your consciousness and we feared you might be unrecoverable. Do you remember what happened when you Uploaded off the asteroid?"

Rilee closed her eyes for a moment until the memories came rushing back, and she reopened them in alarm. "I have critical information for the General Secretary! I must speak with him immediately!"

An expression Rilee couldn't identify flashed across the medic's face. She stood and smiled as she turned to leave the room.

"He left orders that he wanted to speak with you as soon as possible if we managed to restore your consciousness. Let me see if I can track him down. He might have his hands full today of all days. I have to leave you restrained for now, but I'm hopeful you've recovered. If you're still this calm and lucid after an hour, we'll let you loose."

The *today of all days* comment from the medic struck her as odd, but the woman left the room before Rilee could get a question out. Her brain acted like it was a split second out of phase with her body. The sensation was similar to jumping into a new Skin for the first time, but Rilee knew she was riding her personal Pattern because of the small tattoo on her forearm. It featured a circle in the middle which overlapped two additional circles on each side. The symbol had been used by her family for generations to brand the cattle on their land. Rilee had made it a permanent part of her Pattern so she would always be reminded of the simpler, happier times she was fighting to make possible again.

An alert chimed and the wall opposite the bed came alive as a communication screen. A large numeral in the center of the screen counted down from five, and when it reached zero the face of the General Secretary appeared. The man dominated the frame, but Rilee could see into a large room behind him where at least twenty people sat at various workstations. He looked at Rilee, and a tight smile creased his mouth before he spoke.

"You have impeccable timing, but I'm glad we're able to connect. I was worried—"

"I'm sorry to interrupt, sir, but I've got critical information to share with you that I discovered up on Adan's asteroid."

The General Secretary raised his hand to stop Rilee from speaking. "Let me guess—he built transports that can carry huge numbers of people in cryostorage, and he brought offensive nukes into orbit."

Rilee couldn't prevent her jaw from going slack. The Secretary grinned at her reaction and continued to speak.

"There's no great way to tell you this, Rilee. The doctors have been trying to repair your consciousness for almost a year, and an awful lot happened while you were out of action. They would have given up on you long ago, but I ordered them to keep trying until they exhausted every possible chance of recovery."

A year! Rilee found herself unable to breathe. The General Secretary waited before speaking again while she gathered her wits and took a dozen deep breaths to center back on their conversation.

"We learned about the transports a month ago when they showed up on Earth and started to collect people from the West."

"How many people did he collect, sir?"

"Just about all of them. There were a few hundred thousand holdouts who were stubborn like you about staying behind, but Adan managed to gather almost a billion people. He's got them all in cryostorage on his rock. This means the West has ceded Earth to the East. After generations where they fought us at every turn as we tried to preserve the planet for the future, they've now given up on it to go find new worlds to destroy."

"I had feared something like that might be happening when I discovered the transports and cryotubes. I'm sorry I failed you, sir, and that you didn't find out about this until there was nothing that could be done. How did the Central Committee react?"

"The public position was to declare victory. The East now has full control of Earth and can act accordingly. I know you had planned to convince the West to finally work together and save the planet once the Chancellor left, but now you don't have to bother. All of you who remain behind can instead focus your energies toward saving our homeworld.

"The private position, though, was to be furious. If we had known how Adan had made preparations to relocate the entirety of the West, we would have negotiated far harder to have set aside more space for our citizens. I know many of our people feel similarly to you and would have remained behind regardless, but there's no good reason we shouldn't have been able to bring far, far more along with us."

"What about the nukes, sir? I would've bet anything the Committee would declare war based on that type of treaty violation."

"We started to agitate for more information as it became clear how many fighters Adan was building for his ship. He forced the Chancellor to confirm what we've long suspected, Rilee. Earth has been visited on multiple occasions by aliens. I was able to see their ships with my own eyes. The West has them hidden deep underground in that facility you always begged me for permission to infiltrate. They were only small scout craft, but they were armed with offensive weaponry. It was clear to all of us on the Central Committee that if there was a chance of running into violent aliens, it made absolute sense to bring offensive nukes along on our journey. After all, we don't want to be trapped here on this rock alongside Adan and have it be defenseless."

"Wait—are you up on the asteroid right now, sir?"

"Remember, Rilee, you've been all but dead for a year. I said your timing was impeccable because we're actually leaving within the next few days. If you hadn't returned to full consciousness when you did, I would have missed out on this chance to say goodbye. And also, to say thank you. If our society is to have any chance of survival on Earth, I'm confident it will only be due to your personal efforts. I'm supremely grateful you're staying behind to help our people who remain, and I hope to return at some point in the future and discover you beat the odds and succeeded. I'm sure—"

The Secretary paused and looked to his right. Rilee's heart rate spiked when panic filled the man's voice as he spoke to someone offscreen.

"He did what?"

The General Secretary turned back to face the camera, but he disappeared from the screen before saying another word when the connection went dead. A moment later the lights in Rilee's room flipped to red as a klaxon shrieked.

CHAPTER FOURTEEN

We need to sort some stuff out.

Zax made it to the training facility with a few mins to spare. Simulation helmets were arrayed around the compartment, and his pulse quickened at the realization he was getting behind the stick of a spacecraft—even if only for a training drill. Despite many years having passed in actuality, to Zax's mind it had only been a few days since he had flown, and he itched to do so again.

A few stragglers entered the compartment and found seats. The lights dimmed and Kalare appeared on a screen. She was flanked by the Flight Boss on one side and Major Eryn on the other. Zax's fists clenched at the sight of the man who had condemned him to cryostorage. He was grateful their first encounter was via one-way video rather than face-to-face. The Boss spoke first.

"I know all of you have had an initial briefing with the CAG, but I want to stress the importance of what we have ahead of us. The Ship has been attacked repeatedly and vigorously by a force of unknown humans. We've beaten them time and again, and they may have withdrawn permanently since we haven't come across them for a long time. However, it's most likely a threat remains. If they attack when we arrive back at Earth, we plan to overwhelm them and put an end to this. The President has declared that if our homeworld is worth inhabiting, we will pay any price to do so. Mini-Boss—"

The Boss turned to Major Eryn. *Mini-Boss.* Major Eryn had moved up in standing while Zax was in storage. She had already been an influential Omega with her role atop the Pilot Academy, but a promotion to Mini-Boss was acknowledgement that she was likely to earn the top spot and become Flight Boss. Or, at least, the top spot that remained available to Crew given the Ship no longer had a captain and instead operated with a civilian president. She spoke.

"We pulled you out of cryostorage so we can be certain of delivering on that plan. You represent all of the reliable pilot reinforcements we have available. By preparing you for this battle along with our current team of pilots, we are confident we can deploy an overwhelming force if we encounter the humans back at Earth.

"I understand some of you have raised questions about your status and whether you'll remain out of cryostorage when this is all done. You have not been restored to full Crew membership as of now. There's a chance for you to earn that privilege based on your performance in the months ahead."

Major Eryn paused for a moment to let the news sink in before she continued. "By the time we reach Earth, the bottom ten percent of your group will have been cycled back into cryostorage through a special weekly Cull process. The top ten percent will be restored to permanent Crew status. The fate of everyone in-between depends on what we find when we get back to Earth. If the planet is habitable, you will be resettled there. If it remains lifeless, then you'll be returned to cryosleep and given priority for resettlement on the highest quality planets among those we next encounter. I'm going to hand it over to the CAG, and she'll brief you on today's simulated mission."

Zax was not the least bit surprised how the Omegas had created a competition with significant stakes. The Crew had turned its back on all of these pilots when they were first pushed into cryostorage, so there had to be some way of buying back their maximum effort. Full restoration of Crew status would be a valuable prize for many, and Zax was a little shocked by how much it grabbed his own attention. By the way everyone else in his training compartment had leaned forward at Major Eryn's words, Zax wasn't alone in that assessment. Kalare spoke.

"You're all about to participate in the largest battle simulation the Ship has ever executed. We're speaking with you via video because we've created dozens of new training compartments around the Ship, and there are just about ten thousand of you who will participate in this first evaluation.

"The rules are simple. You're each on your own, and we've removed the capability for direct pilot-to-pilot communication to ensure there's no coordination among you. Battle until only one of you remains. You have sixty secs to prepare before we start."

Zax reached beneath his seat for his helmet. He slipped it on and was immersed into the fighter simulation environment. As Maverick for his Pilot Academy class, Zax had once proved he was among the best of his peers. He assumed many of the pilots he was about to face had not been similarly skilled. If they were, they most likely wouldn't have wound up in cryostorage. After all, most pilots who were that successful didn't turn around and make wild claims about conspiracy theories centered around powerful Omegas.

All systems checked out in his virtual spacecraft, and Zax held his breath as the mission clock counted down the secs until the competition started. The clock hit zero, and his threat board lit up with a maelstrom of targeting details. Ten thousand fighters in a simulation where every single one was an opponent was a nearly impossible situation for the threat system to process. He tuned it out in favor of operating on his own instincts.

Zax zoomed his fighter away from the morass of competitors out to the periphery of the battle. While doing so, he identified three main profiles of pilots in the competition. The largest group was made up of those who furiously engaged every single target possible. There were a few in that group who stood out as being skilled, but many ended up dying off solely because the sheer volume of craft made it impossible to manage the tactical situation as a lone individual.

The next group, smaller but still significant, was made up of pilots who were stepping away from the heart of the battle like Zax. They engaged as needed when they encountered other craft but appeared intent on observing the situation rather than diving in.

The last group was smallest, though large enough to be noticeable. Pilots who did nothing. They merely sat exposed without moving and waited until someone came along and took them out without offering any resistance or attempts at evasion. Zax was puzzled by these people at first until he remembered Major Eryn's words. The bottom ten percent of pilots were going to be sent back to cryostorage. The willing target dummies must be people who had already made up their mind and actively wanted to place themselves into that group. For whatever reason, they must have concluded life on the Ship wasn't anything they were interested in participating in any longer.

A cluster of these sacrificial lambs was torn to shreds in front of him and triggered an idea for Zax. He navigated towards the tight cloud of wreckage created by their destruction and, while avoiding any chunks with enough mass to damage his craft, glided into its center. He matched his velocity and vector with the debris around him before shutting down his engine.

In fighter engagements, speed and maneuverability were considered to be a pilot's lifeblood. Zax had now forfeited those tools in favor of camouflage. He was betting the remains of other fighters were becoming so prevalent they would cease to draw close attention, and he could hide in relative plain sight among them. It was an all or nothing bet because he would be unable to restore his engines and gain velocity fast enough to avoid anyone who might identify and target his craft.

Zax sat back and observed the threat board. Min after min his decision appeared even better. No sooner would he identify a pilot who exhibited above average skill than that pilot's craft would wind up shattered by a random opponent who got lucky. There were just too many threats in too small a volume of space for anyone to survive for long.

For almost sixty mins the pattern continued to play out until it changed like a switch had flipped. Some critical density of active fighters was crossed that left few enough combatants so the true skill of pilots meant the difference for long-term survival. The numbers then dwindled faster and faster until there were only a few hundred still in the battle. Zax waited for the ideal window to leave his hiding place and reengage in combat.

Finally, Zax settled on the top ten remaining combatants who exhibited the most tactical ability and piloting skill. He configured his threat system to prioritize their location and activities over all others and fired up his engines. He drew unwanted attention right away, but he had appropriately timed his emergence to avoid anyone being close enough to engage before he could reestablish sufficient velocity.

Five. Ten. Fifteen. Zax tore a path of destruction through the remaining fighters and cut down not only the chaff who had zero chance of winning the battle, but also half of those pilots he had identified as significant threats. While he was doing so, another of the most talented pilots went on a tear and managed to clean up all of the remaining combatants.

There were only two of them left!

The space around them was littered with debris, and Zax and the other pilot were the only signs of life. They weaved and dodged for a few mins to feel each other out, but each feint was met with an effective counter. They were evenly matched, and Zax began to worry about his inability to destroy his final competitor until the other pilot gave too wide a berth to a large piece of wreckage. It was the slightest of mistakes as it gave Zax a fractionally better angle of attack, but it appeared sufficient. He nudged his craft onto the appropriate vector and a few secs later thrilled at the prospect of winning the contest. His opponent continued to fly such that it was clear the pilot had not anticipated how Zax had gained a definitive advantage.

Zax was only a moment away from engaging the target with a shower of plasma when he was shocked by his threat board's squawking. The craft he pursued disintegrated in front of him, but he had not yet fired a shot. A split sec later, the same fate befell Zax. His craft held together just long enough for him to identify the cause. Another pilot had adopted the same camouflage technique Zax had used earlier but had exhibited far more patience. Not only had the fighter remained hidden until there were only two other competitors remaining, but the pilot hadn't engaged until those competitors crossed a targeting vector where a sneak attack with zero warning was possible.

The simulation ended and Zax's attention returned to the training compartment. He was about to remove his helmet when a light flashed to signal an incoming private message. He accepted and Kalare's face filled his viewscreen.

"Well done, Zax. I'm sure you're disappointed about getting beaten by your own strategy there at the end, but it's still impressive for you to have outlasted almost all of the other pilots. The vast majority of them have extensive real-world combat experience you never had a chance to gain."

Zax puffed up with pride at Kalare's praise. She continued.

"Meet me in the mess hall for dinner tonight. We need to sort some stuff out."

The connection went dead before Zax could say a word. Kalare's tone hadn't been the warmest, but he was thrilled that she reached out to him after she had actively avoided him yesterday. He quickly forgot about his success in the simulator as his mind was instead flooded with thoughts of what it would be like to reconnect with his best friend.

Correction—the woman who used to be a girl he was best friends with.

CHAPTER FIFTEEN

So I've been told.

The mess hall at dinnertime was as annoyingly loud and boisterous as it had been at breakfast. Zax barely noticed as his excitement about spending time with Kalare made him immune to anything the current Ship could throw at him. Well—*almost* anything. Finding Aleron seated next to Kalare stopped Zax cold. He debated turning around and walking out, but his old nemesis looked up and caught his eye while Zax worked through his indecisiveness. The man hadn't aged a bit in twelve years. Aleron maintained a neutral expression and waved Zax over as he leaned over and whispered to Kalare.

Kalare looked up as Zax approached and a panoply of emotions spilled across her face. The one that remained at the end was an apprehension that mirrored the tightness in Zax's chest. Aleron stood and extended his hand in greeting. Zax shook it mindlessly while never taking his eyes off Kalare's face. Aleron bent over and kissed the top of her head before speaking.

"Welcome back, Zax. I hope you two enjoy catching up. I'll see you back at our quarters when you're done, Kalare."

Aleron's physical intimacy with Kalare combined with his parting words struck Zax with the force of a plasma cannon. If a chair hadn't been in a position where he could collapse into it, Zax might have tottered over and crashed to the deck. His eyes remained locked on the surface of the table as they threatened to overflow with tears.

"I'm sorry, Zax."

The words were barely a whisper, but they broke the spell. Zax sniffled, blinked to clear his vision, and then choked back his emotions enough to raise his head and meet Kalare's gaze. Up close her face was as beautiful as it had always been, but it was different than he so vividly remembered. Some combination of age and responsibility had dulled the spark that had always warmed his heart. She stared at him unblinkingly until it became uncomfortable and then she broke into one of her radiant smiles.

"I can't believe it's really you, Zax. This is the first time I've interacted with someone I knew before they went into cryostorage. You look exactly the same as I remember. Exactly."

"So I've been told."

Zax had tried to modulate his tone, but it was clear from Kalare's flinch that his words landed more harshly than intended. He took a deep breath before continuing.

"I'm sorry, Kalare. I'm not trying to lash out at you. You've done nothing but be my friend for years. Seeing Aleron with you...like that...is hard. You two share quarters now?"

Kalare looked down for a sec before replying.

"We've been together for a few years. I had stayed away from him for a long time after you were Culled. It was too painful to see him because it made me think about you. He gave me space but persisted until the pain about losing you faded."

The words hit Zax like a punch. He must have given an outward expression of his feelings because Kalare's tone changed as she continued.

"I'm sorry, Zax. What did you expect me to do? You were gone. I had no reason to believe I'd ever see you again."

"I don't know what I expected. I truly don't. I understand intellectually how you've lived twelve years of your life without me, but it still feels like it was just yesterday we were standing in here talking about having breakfast together the next day. I look at you and my heart feels like I know you, but I realize I have to convince myself that I don't. Not anymore. Maybe you can help me try?"

Kalare's eyes overflowed with warmth. "I'd be happy to help you better know the person I am now.

Should I start at the beginning and move forwards or start at the end and move backwards? I don't know. Starting at the beginning might be easier, but starting at the end is where more of the interesting stuff has happened." Kalare paused and closed her eyes as she took an exaggerated deep breath before continuing. "Well, one big change is I've become much better at not going off on verbal floods like I used to all the time. What would *you* like to learn about first?"

Zax was disappointed. He had embraced the familiar feeling of breathlessness that had taken hold as Kalare had started to speak faster and faster before catching herself. It made sense she would have worked to remove the tic as she got older and rose through the ranks, but it was just one more sign of how much the world had changed without him.

"Why don't you tell me about how you got to be CAG?"

Kalare smiled. "I came out of the Academy at the top of my class and picked a fighter role. My first couple of years were tricky as I had a squad leader who just didn't like me very much. I got desperate and reached out to Major Eryn for some guidance and we ended up getting along great. For whatever reason, she really understood me and coached me on how the politics work in the fighter pilot community. With her guidance, I got to be as good at the interpersonal stuff as I've always been at the actual piloting."

Zax held up his hand to interrupt Kalare. "Wait—did you just say you've become good at politics?

I don't think you even understood what the word meant back when I knew you."

Kalare grinned wider. "I know! Crazy, isn't it? I don't know what changed, but I set my mind to winning and it started to happen more often. I kept rising through the ranks and that accelerated even faster as we engaged the human fighters more frequently. My battle tactics had the best results against the humans and got me a lot of attention. I'm sure both the Major and the Boss were pulling some strings as well, but I feel pretty confident that whatever influence they had was only possible because I was so successful."

Kalare's mention of the Boss's likely role in her career ascent should have sent Zax into an emotional tailspin given the circumstances. Her relationship with the man had always been a source of significant friction in their friendship, but Zax had spent the day mentally preparing himself to not let anything sidetrack their reunion. He was dying to know if she had ever challenged the man about why he banished Zax to cryosleep, but had convinced himself that topic could wait until their friendship was returned to a more stable footing. Kalare continued her story.

"A couple of years ago we lost the CAG in a battle against the humans, and they picked me to replace him! It was pretty surprising because a few other people who were a lot more experienced got skipped over, but almost everyone believed I was the best choice at the time. We haven't had any defeats in battle since I took over, so I think I've managed to win everyone else over as well."

"Wow, Kalare. That's incredible. I'm not surprised you've been so successful, of course, but it really sounds like you've totally dedicated yourself. That's a big change from when I knew you. I dreamed of being CAG myself, of course, but seeing you get there is the next best thing. Maybe if I put my head down and focus, I can regain Crew status like Major Eryn announced earlier and then have a shot at following in your footsteps."

Kalare opened her mouth to reply, but paused. She closed her eyes to instead deal with an incoming message via her Plug. After a few moments, she opened them and spoke.

"Sorry, Zax, but I've got to leave. That was the Boss and he needs me."

Kalare stood as she rushed to gather her empty plates and trash. Zax stood as well to say goodbye. He wanted to give Kalare a hug, but, as she came around the table, she held her tray in front of her with both hands. He guessed it was a coincidence and not an intentional tactic to avoid physical contact, but Zax was disappointed. He smiled at her as warmly as he could muster as he said farewell.

"Thanks for talking with me. I know you must be super busy, so I appreciate you making the time. Do you think we could do it again soon? There's more I'd like to ask you about."

"Yeah, Zax, that would be nice. It's great to have you back. I'll contact you again soon and will look forward to spending more time together next time."

Zax hoped her words were genuine and not just a polite response, but he was unable to divine any further clues from her facial expression. She smiled one last time and then was gone. No sooner had she walked away and Zax had sat back down to eat his meal than someone flopped into the seat next to him. Mase.

"Zax—I've done it. You're not going to believe what I've managed to unlock!"

CHAPTER SIXTEEN

You're going to love it!

Zax sighed and didn't bother to mask his disappointment about Mase's arrival. The conversation with Kalare had drained him emotionally and he didn't have any energy left for pretense. Just as when he was younger, the man either didn't pick up on any of the non-verbal cues or ignored them and instead barreled ahead.

"Last year I hacked my way into an AI system filled with various log files. The ones I could access at first were pretty boring and benign. Different Omegas from the last five thousand years giving updates on Ship activities. The sheer volume of it all made it impossible to delve too deep to find any interesting stuff. What really caught my attention was a group of files with a second level of unbreakable encryption."

The man stopped speaking and stared at Zax as if he expected feedback on how interesting the story was so far. Against his better judgment, Zax half-smiled and nodded for him to continue. He instantly regretted the decision because Mase went off on a five min dissertation on the relative strengths and weaknesses of the different encryption algorithms employed by the various Artificial Intelligence systems across the Ship. Zax took advantage of the time to finish his meal as he tried to give the illusion he was paying attention. Once he was done eating he interrupted.

"I'm sorry, Mase. It's been a long day. All I want to do is crash in my bunk. Is there a short version of this story I can have right now, and maybe you can give me all of the details some other time?"

Zax had been afraid he might hurt the man's feelings, but Mase's only reaction was a quick smile before he spoke.

"I finally figured out how to crack the encryption. They are the personal log files of the man who built the Ship and was its first leader. They go all the way back to the time before the Ship left Earth."

Zax's mouth hung open as he took a few moments to process what Mase had shared. "What? There isn't any history of that period anywhere in the Ship's records."

"I know. I couldn't believe what I was looking at. I had almost given up on breaking the encryption until I found a document with the information I needed. I was frustrated because I could have sworn I had checked everywhere for clues. It must have been there all along and yet somehow I missed it."

"Mase—please shut up about the stupid encryption! Tell me more about these logs. How do you know for sure who they belong to?"

"I know because he states over and over again who he is. He goes into great detail about his thoughts and his conversations and all of the activities going on back then. He was intentionally creating a permanent record of what had transpired. And it starts all the way back around the time when they first started building the Ship. He describes the trip he made from Earth out to find the asteroid to build it on. It took them more than a year to travel a few hundred million klicks. Can you imagine that?"

Zax found himself wildly conflicted. Mase had discovered a trove of fascinating information that would be exciting to explore, but did Zax really want to immerse himself in it? If the logs were encrypted, there was likely sensitive material in there the builder didn't want discovered. Zax had already spent too many years carrying around information he had to hide from others and couldn't imagine any situation where he'd want to deal with all of that again. He stood.

"Congratulations, Mase, about this pretty amazing work. I don't think I'm interested in learning anything more right now, though. Thanks for trusting me with your secret, but I just can't handle the burden of it. I just sat out the last twelve years because I had to go shooting off my mouth about other big secrets. I don't need to get exposed to any more of them where I might be tempted to do the same once again."

"Zax—it shows what happened to Earth before the Ship left. We're going to find a dead planet when we get there."

Zax paused. Deep down he knew the right answer was to simply walk away. Zax didn't know anything the rest of the Ship wouldn't learn in just a few months anyway. Mase's expression hinted there was much more explosive information to be learned, but Zax didn't need that in his life. Heads down. He needed to be heads down and focused on getting back into the Crew.

Zax almost turned and walked away. Almost. Then he considered for a moment what Kalare might advise if she was present. It wasn't that thought which gave him pause, but instead the vision that immediately followed—Kalare returning to her quarters and falling into the arms of Aleron. Twelve years in cryostorage had robbed Zax of his best friend. Even if she was genuine in wanting to repair and continue their relationship, it could never be the same again.

Even his friendship with Mase was forever altered by the Cull. Zax recognized the boy's mannerisms in the man who sat next to him, but it was not the same person who Zax had become friends with through their shared life together in the Academy. Mase had gone on to have many experiences that Zax would never fully comprehend. The lost years would always represent an insurmountable gulf between them.

Did Zax really want to go back to living in isolation, focused on nothing but getting ahead? Even that life was not guaranteed any longer. Being a member of the Crew had been robbed from him, and there was no guarantee he'd ever get a spot back on the Leaderboard again. He might fight like crazy for the next few months only to fall short and wind up back in cryostorage. If Mase was correct, there would be no re-settlement on Earth for anyone. He would be Culled for a second time only to wake up on some unknown colony years in the future. Or perhaps never wake up at all, given how the condition of the Ship was on such a downward spiral.

With all of the uncertainty, Zax concluded there was no real downside in seeing what Mase had discovered. He was already living on borrowed time.

"OK, Mase, let's check out what you've got."

The man beamed at him. "Great! This would be easier if your Plug was working. Let's find someplace private where I can hook up to a projector and show you. I've got everything queued up to the part right before they leave Earth. You're going to love it!"

Zax wholeheartedly doubted Mase's conclusion, but he stood and followed the man nonetheless.

CHAPTER SEVENTEEN

Why do you have to take this drastic step?

"What the hell is going on, Adan?"

The General Secretary was displayed on the huge panorama that Adan's engineers had perfected over the last few months prior to departure. The flight operations center Adan designed was his favorite space on the starship. One of the three hundred square meter windows looked out into the void and a second opposite overlooked the flight hangar with its myriad fighters, scouts, and transports. The ship also had a traditional bridge where Adan could have full operational control, but he preferred to spend his time in flight operations if he wasn't out on the stick of one of his amazing fighters. Adan would have given anything to be piloting rather than dealing with the odious leader of the East, but it was time to tie up some loose ends prior to departure.

"Whatever are you talking about, Mr. Secretary?"

The General Secretary's face shaded towards a deep crimson, and he appeared as if he might have a stroke. Before he could reply the Chancellor spoke up from the other side of the compartment.

"Adan—be polite. There's no sport in playing around with him at this point. We've clearly bested the Secretary, so let's just put him out of his misery rather than prolong this unpleasantness."

The words *shut up* perched on the tip of Adan's tongue. As far as he was concerned, their imminent departure from Earth meant he was now in complete command. He had kowtowed to the Chancellor to secure the resources and support he needed during construction, but their deal had been explicit. Going forward she was a passenger and therefore a guest in his operations center. Nothing more.

Adan glanced past the Chancellor to the woman's Chief of Staff who stood right behind her. Jania stared at him like she was sizing up the potential for conflict. There would be a time to let the leader of the West and her lackey know her title and all it conveyed had become null and void, but that moment had not yet arrived. It didn't mean he had to follow the woman's wishes, though. Especially when it came to dealing with the General Secretary however he saw fit.

The enmity Adan harbored for the East and its leader had many sources. The heart of the matter, of course, was the East's willingness to give up the freedom of their physical bodies to exist instead in some government-controlled, virtual reality. Like everyone else in the West, Adan wanted no part of that harsh conservation measure which the East sought to impose as their preferred solution for saving the Earth. Not only was the approach far too blunt for his taste, Adan also believed it was mostly window dressing that would extend the planet's habitability by a few measly decades at best. Even if the East was right, what was the point of saving Earth if it required one to adopt their collectivist mindset that enforced a dogmatic equality and prevented society's best from earning superior rewards in exchange for extraordinary contributions?

More important to Adan, especially as it related to the General Secretary himself, was the degree to which the man had once tortured Markev. Long before he worked for Adan, Markev had been captured during a mission to steal the secrets behind the East's Upload technology. His aide's horrific stories about his treatment at the hands of the General Secretary had long ago removed whatever semblance of humanity Adan might have otherwise been willing to ascribe to the man. The East's leader deserved retribution for his past crimes, and Adan wanted his most trusted and respected lieutenant to deliver the payback.

"Markev—would you like to explain the situation to the General Secretary?"

Adan's bodyguard pushed his shoulders back and strode close to the screen before speaking. It was almost as if he wanted to deliver his words as intimately as possible.

"Mr. Secretary—I hear quite a bit of tumult happening on your end. Your people are no doubt trying to understand how all of the hatches in your facility have been secured and your outbound communications severed. You should advise your team they may as well halt their efforts as they're wasting their time. We've isolated you from the rest of the spaceship. We've also jammed *all* of the wireless frequencies you might use for communication or *any* other purposes. You're all about to die, and you may as well go peacefully rather than run around in a panic for no purpose."

Markev's words hit home and the color drained from the Secretary's face. The man's Adam's apple bounced as he swallowed a couple of times before speaking.

"Madam Chancellor—why are you going back on our agreement? Isn't it enough you cheated us and evacuated all of your citizens while leaving the vast majority of ours behind? Why do you have to take this drastic step? If this has all been a charade and you never had any intention of taking us with you, then just send me and my people back down to the surface. The West is leaving Earth behind so there's no reason you shouldn't just let us go back and help our people save the planet."

The Chancellor slowly shook her head. "There you go again. You mention us leaving and the idea of saving the planet in the same sentence like the two are related. You do realize that's the type of sanctimony that has brought us to this point, right? We've spent decades fighting, and it always comes down to you wanting to blame the West for the state of the planet. You act all high and mighty with your blather about *ecological footprints* while you try to impose your belief system on us. Meanwhile, you're out there killing and torturing our people as if you stood any chance of swaying us to your perspectives through intimidation and violence. We always knew there would be a technological solution to the Earth's situation, and here we are today standing on it. The difference is that while the East obsessed about saving a random rock floating through space, we were focused on saving the *species*. And we have. Humanity will live on out among the stars. And not just on one rock, but on hundreds of them."

Markev turned back from watching the Chancellor speak and addressed the leader of the East again. "In a few moments, we'll detonate the explosives built into the foundation that binds your facility to the asteroid. It won't kill you, but instead you'll float free and be cut off from our artificial gravity and life support. That won't matter for long, though, because we've shaped the charges to impart enough momentum that within two hours you'll re-enter the atmosphere and burn up. You and your people don't have to suffer and wait for the end, if you prefer not to. We've got weapons targeted that can give you a much cleaner and faster death once we've cut you free from the ship. It's your choice, sir. What say you?"

The compartment was silent as everyone waited for the man to reply. He turned to face someone off camera and spoke softly with his mouth covered, so it was impossible to hear his words or read his lips. After a few moments of back and forth, he faced the camera and spoke quietly as his shoulders slumped.

"Use the weapons."

Adan smiled. "A coward to the end, I see. I'm not surprised after the numerous stories I've heard from people like Markev here who suffered at your hands. I'm happy to give you the quick death you've requested even though it's not the one you deserve. There's one last thing I want you to witness before we send you on your way, though."

Markev spun around to look back at his boss with his mouth open in surprise. Adan had never informed his aide about the final component of his agreement with the Chancellor. Markev was enthusiastic about killing off the East's leadership after the abuse they had subjected him to, but Adan knew the man might have viewed the next step as one too far. Rather than risk having to debate the point, he had kept it hidden. Adan called out the order.

"Prepare to launch the missiles."

CHAPTER EIGHTEEN

This is my ship and these are my rules.

"General Secretary—there's another reason why your request to return to the surface can't be honored. Earth will be dead before you are. In fact, you're only still breathing because we want you to bear witness to that fact. I know you're aware we brought nuclear weapons on board, and the justification we gave you with regards to our needs for self-defense was a valid one. However, we have a more immediate need for the nukes and that is to wipe every trace of the East from existence. I will soon launch enough missiles to consume Earth with fire for years. When there's nothing left to burn, the radiation will leave the planet lifeless for a hundred millennia."

"Adan—you can't do this!"

Markev's shout echoed across the compartment. Adan paused and turned his attention to his bodyguard. The man flashed their secret signal to suggest Adan pause for a moment to think. Adan shook his head.

"I'm not being rash, Markev. This is a well-thought-out plan. Why do you have any problem with it? After all the East has done to you in the past, why do you want to extend them any mercy? They're barely human at this point given the way they treat their bodies like clothes to be swapped and discarded."

Markev approached and spoke in smooth, measured tones. "The General Secretary and everyone associated with him needs to die, yes. The people down below are innocent bystanders in all of this. Their beliefs are different from ours, but they aren't the ones trying to force them down our throats. That direction comes from the man up on the screen. Kill him, yes, but not nine billion innocents. They'll all die in a few years anyway. Why not just let nature do its work and reclaim the planet?"

"I genuinely wish I could avoid this next step, Markev, but I feel I have no choice. Are you familiar with the story of Cortez?"

"Sir—what does that have to do with anything?"

"Answer the question. Yes, or no?"

"No."

Adan turned back to the General Secretary who was watching from the screen. "We haven't forgotten about you Mr. Secretary. It's probably good for you to hear this as well.

"Now, Markev. You're worried I'm being hasty and acting impulsively out of pure revenge. The rationale the Chancellor advocated is precisely that simple and crass. The truth is actually much different for me and payback is not my driving force. Instead, I see the death of billions as a sacrifice that is horrific and yet still required to save the rest of the species.

"Back to Cortez. The man was an explorer in the sixteenth century who sailed across the Atlantic to conquer newly discovered lands. Despite his force being technologically superior, most of Cortez's men had never experienced battle and were tempted to flee home in the face of the ferocious natives they encountered. Cortez burned his fleet to present his men with a simple choice—fight or die. They fought and they won."

All of the engineers in the compartment quietly observed the scene. Adan wasn't particularly worried about Markev as he was confident about bringing him around to the proper perspective. His main audience was instead those members of his crew who manned the various workstations. They needed to be witness to this act and understand its significance, so they could spread the message far and wide. There was no more home. There was no turning back. Humanity's only direction was forward, regardless of what challenges might be encountered along that path. Adan turned his attention back to Markev who asked a question.

"Sir—I understand what you're trying to accomplish, but can't we figure out a better approach than wholesale murder?"

The Chancellor spoke before Adan could reply.

"Why are we dragging this out, Adan? Can't you get your boy to shut up so we can get this over with."

Markev possessed stunning speed for someone so large and bulky. In a flash, he crossed the few paces that separated him from the Chancellor and placed the older woman in a crushing choke hold.

Jania's reflexes were fast, but she was still a half-second late in her response. She pulled a weapon hidden in the small of her back and aimed it at Markev's head.

"She gets hurt, you die," spat the Chancellor's Chief of Staff.

"Whoa! Everyone calm down!" Adan threw his arms up. He walked towards Markev slowly with his palms outstretched. It was a bizarre tableau in front of him, with the Chancellor's fingers clawing at Markev's massive bicep as her face reddened from the stress and lack of oxygen. Adan needed to defuse the situation fast.

"Markev—you don't have to let her go, but let her breathe a little. She's tough as nails, but she's still old. Let's not kill her by accident, OK?"

The bodyguard's facial expression didn't change, but his arm relaxed ever so slightly. The Chancellor was still in distress, but her color stabilized as she was allowed just enough oxygen to stay conscious.

"OK. Good. Thank you. Can I come closer and talk privately?"

Markev nodded.

Once Adan got close enough, he whispered. "Markev—what's going on? Why are you doing this?"

"This isn't you, Adan. I don't know what's happened over the last few years, but something has changed. We never should have agreed to work with any of these monsters because nothing good has come of it. We could have built all of this on our own and then just left them behind to squabble over a dying planet."

"Markev—I know you haven't agreed with all of my choices along the way. I'm sorry, but I've always tried to take the path I felt gave us the best chance to save the species. That goal is all that matters to me. I don't take the sacrifice of nine billion people lightly. This decision is the hardest I've ever made, but it feels like the right one. We don't know what challenges we're going to face as we head into the unknown. Everyone on board needs to know with certainty there's no turning back. Without that sense of finality, there will be too many opportunities to second-guess the decision to leave. Without absolute focus around a singular purpose, humanity will die. I'm convinced. Please trust me."

Adan watched as Markev processed his words. His facial expression remained stoic until it shifted almost imperceptibly. The giant shifted his arm position so instead of choking the older woman he held her upright and prevented her collapse to the deck. Jania stepped away and lowered her weapon, and Markev pivoted his body to gently guide the Chancellor into a chair. The woman broke into a coughing fit as Markev turned and walked out of the compartment.

After nearly a minute of coughing, the Chancellor calmed and Adan addressed her.

"My apologies for his unfortunate reaction, Madam Chancellor. You were never in any danger. If he was going to kill you, he would have done it before you had a moment to know what was happening."

Adan turned to Jania. "And you would have been dead before the Chancellor's body hit the deck if that was his intent. I know this event makes you feel justified in having smuggled that weapon on board my spaceship, but I need to take it from you right now. You live under my protection, and I refuse to have any weapons in the hands of people who I have not explicitly granted permission."

Jania turned to look at the Chancellor and Adan spoke again much more sharply.

"Don't look at her. This is my ship and these are my rules. If you don't like it, there's an airlock nearby, and I'd be more than happy to send you on your way."

There was fire in her eyes, but Jania held out her arm and placed the weapon into Adan's outstretched palm. After ensuring it couldn't accidentally discharge, he tucked it into a pocket and turned back to the huge panorama screen.

"Well, Mr. Secretary, I'm sorry to have taken as long as we have with all of this. It was never the intent to draw out your suffering quite this much. There was one important fact I hadn't shared yet before I got interrupted. I want to be certain you hear it lest you nurture any false hope. I had earlier dispatched craft armed with nukes to Mars as well as the asteroid belt. Looking at how things have taken longer than expected here, those settlements of yours have already been destroyed. It's time for you to witness the same fate befall your citizens down below."

With the intervening drama, the General Secretary had been granted sufficient time to regain his composure. He appeared remarkably calm for a man who was about to watch nine billion of his citizens die before facing his own death. His mouth formed into a tight smile as he spoke.

"I promise you'll regret this."

The giant display faded to black as the Secretary cut the connection. Adan turned to the woman who sat at the weapons station.

"Launch the missiles."

CHAPTER NINETEEN

How will I be able to control them?

Humanity's first home still dominated Adan's view out of the flight operations exterior panorama, though the planet had become unrecognizable. It was forty-eight hours after missiles had rained down, and the blue and white marble was blanketed in gray and black roiling clouds of smoke and ash. A red glow emanated through the dense cover and evidenced the all-consuming fires scouring away any evidence of humankind's short tenancy. Perhaps after millions of years some new form of intelligent life might arise on the planet once again, but it would be radically different having evolved out of the hellscape of radioactive fallout that would blanket the surface for millennia.

The future of the human species was out among the stars, and no one understood and appreciated that more than the people in the flight operations center. The group of engineers Adan had recruited and nurtured over the course of spaceship construction were hard at work making final preparations to leave Earth behind forever. They were the best minds humanity had ever produced, and he was confident they would lead the species towards long-term survival.

The Chancellor strode in trailed, as always, by her Chief of Staff. Adan stood and directed them towards the small conference room attached to the operations center. He fell into step behind Jania and closed the hatch behind them as the women sat. He joined them at the table and kept a neutral expression on his face. Jania spoke first.

"How are preparations going for departure?"

"All systems are checking out as expected. We will depart the system in three days."

"Excellent. All we have left to finalize is our first destination."

"I thought I had made it clear, Jania. We've picked our destination."

"Understood, but the Chancellor and I have a change in plans. Our experts reviewed the astronomical data you collected from all of your test flights, and they've drawn different conclusions than your people. They've identified a better path."

Adan paused to consider his response. He was surprised the two of them were going to keep pushing the limits of his authority. Especially after the forcefulness with which he had treated Jania when he confiscated her weapon. He pushed back even harder.

"It's interesting your team has some different opinions. Regardless, we're not changing our course. Direct your *experts* to send their analysis to my navigation team, and we'll see if there's anything we can do to help them understand where they're mistaken."

Jania looked at the Chancellor. The older woman gave an almost imperceptible shake of her head before she turned to Adan and spoke.

"Good enough, Adan. Thanks for hearing us out. We're likely going to be on this rock together for quite a while, so it really doesn't matter whether or not one course might be marginally better than another. Frankly there's more pressing information I wanted to cover. Disturbing information."

Adan gestured for the Chancellor to continue, and she took a deep breath before doing so.

"There's quite a bit of unrest stirring among the general populace. I don't have a lot of concrete details to share, but I'm hearing enough chatter that I thought you needed to know. We appear to have misjudged the reaction to your missile strike. I imagined the majority of people would have been excited about your actions while the rest would be neutral, but the reality is quite different. There's a small minority who are pleased about your destruction of the East, but a much larger number are quite agitated about the horror you unleashed down below."

The Chancellor stared at Adan unblinkingly once she was done and waited for his reaction. He took a few moments to roll options around in his mind. It was clear she was attempting to portray an overall air of helpfulness, but her repeated reference to the missile strikes as being solely Adan's decision struck him as being intentional and inflammatory. He chose to start with a non-antagonistic response.

"Thank you for sharing this information with me, Chancellor. I'd hate to start our long journey together with people being agitated. I have to admit some confusion, though. We decided together to start out with almost everyone who wasn't critical for launch in cryostorage. You asked that we not force any of the five hundred thousand people you sponsored into cryosleep, and I agreed to that request. If these are all people you recruited for this mission, why aren't you able to exert better control over them?"

The Chancellor fixed Adan with a warm smile. She was amping up the grandmotherly charm she had deployed on a few prior occasions.

"I've learned a lot in my time as a leader, Adan. Now I know you've run many successful companies, so I'm not trying to suggest you're new to the concept of leadership. From my perspective, though, that type of private sector experience doesn't always translate into governmental success. If anything, it will often get in the way of it. Please hear me out and understand I'm just trying to help you be as successful as possible in your new role. The key lesson I'm applying by not speaking up is that it must always be crystal clear who's in charge. All of these people have taken their direction from me for their entire lives. If I start trying to shape their behavior now, they will fall back into those old, comfortable patterns. We need a clean break from our old world and our old patterns so there's no doubt you're in charge now."

"I appreciate the guidance, Madam Chancellor. It still seems like I should be able to somehow leverage your relationship with these people. I don't have any direct connection to them at all. How will I be able to control them?"

The Chancellor laughed warmly rather than mockingly. "Welcome to politics, Adan. I don't know how much you're aware of my early career, but I came into power as a relative neophyte. I spent half of my first decade trying to answer the question you just posed. It was pretty damned rocky most of that time and I made a ton of mistakes, but I think I got better."

"Five years? We don't have five years to get this smoothed out, ma'am. We may very well encounter violent aliens within days of starting our journey. We need this society to be functioning at top performance from the moment we make our first jump."

The Chancellor sat back and stared at the overhead with her hand under her chin. Jania watched the scene unfold with a neutral expression. The Chief of Staff had become much better at hiding her thoughts since the first time Adan had met with her and her boss years earlier. He had decided on that fateful day to make a deal with them and had done so knowing full well he was playing with fire. He suspected the Chancellor was about to reveal the trap he had long anticipated and waited for her to do so. Finally, she spoke.

"There is one idea that comes to mind, Adan. I know this isn't what we always agreed upon, so I won't be surprised if your first instinct is to say no. There are probably other ways we can solve this problem, but I know time is critical. I'm just trying to think of what gives us the best chance for success.

"What if we changed the leadership structure? Today you're acting under the total authority inherited from being the captain of this vessel you've built. We don't have to change that. You could remain in full command of the spaceship and all of the engineers you have crewing it. What we could change, though, would be to restore me to my historical role as the official head of state. I could deal with the headaches of leading the general populace so you could focus on more interesting and rewarding pursuits."

"That's an interesting idea, Madam Chancellor. Thank you. One question—if I'm in charge of the ship and its crew and you're in charge of everything else, who has ultimate authority?"

"Good observation, Adan. There can only be one person with final decision-making power. Given the problems we are trying to solve, I will suggest it should be me. We can just transfer the command structure from Earth up here. You will run your spaceship and lead the people who work for you, but I will be the commander-in-chief with final authority. I had thought I was stepping away from that kind of role, but it has been an effective structure that served our people well for decades. If you think it might be the best thing for us to do now, I'd be willing to continue. I'm guessing deep down you don't have any interest in being a politician. You want to run your ship and explore and find us new worlds to call home. Maybe it would be best if you let me worry about everything else."

There it was. The trap was set. Adan had expected there would be a power struggle eventually but had thought it more likely to rear its head quite a bit further into their journey. Both women stared at him waiting for a response, and he focused on not revealing his true feelings.

"How very gracious of you, Madam Chancellor. I understand how much you've been looking forward to retirement and no longer carrying the burden of so much responsibility. I would like to evaluate this plan with some of my advisors before we discuss it any further."

"Of course, Adan." The Chancellor stood to leave as did Jania. "Oh—there was one other item I meant to share with you. I know you were upset with Jania about the weapon she smuggled aboard. I've made it clear to her how much I disapprove of her having done that. I share your belief that we should keep weapons out of the hands of anyone who shouldn't have them. The thought of any form of armed insurrection is quite worrisome. Unfortunately, I've learned there are rumors of hidden caches of additional weapons. I don't know anything about numbers as these are just rumors, but I have to imagine your security was tight enough there couldn't be very many. Right?"

The old woman delivered this "news" with a glint in her eye, and the intended message landed loud and clear to Adan. If he didn't step into the Chancellor's trap of his own volition, she was going to force him into it at gunpoint.

CHAPTER TWENTY

I don't see what choice we have.

Adan walked to the dojo unsure whether Markev would show up for their weekly sparring match. He hadn't seen his assistant in the three days since the man had stormed out of the flight operations center. The only way two such headstrong individuals had managed to work together for so long was by taking regular opportunities to blow off steam and beat the crap out of each other. If anyone missed their appointment it was almost always Adan who begged off from being too busy, so he assumed his bodyguard would most likely be there.

As expected, Markev was already present with his hulking form bulked up further by the sparring pads he had encased himself in. Adan followed suit and within a few minutes the two men bowed to each other from across the circle.

Markev charged, and it was clear from the ferocity of his attack that Adan was in for punishment. He dodged the first couple of blows until a roundhouse kick connected with his chin and sent him sprawling against the bulkhead. Markev raced at him to deliver a forearm smash to the face, but Adan ducked at the last moment and landed a flurry of punches to the side of the giant's body where the padding was thinnest. The man gasped from the blows, and Adan ducked past him to get back into the sparring circle. He spat and found it was mostly blood. He pointed at the splotch on the deck and smiled across the ring at Markev as the man gathered himself up again.

"It's going to be one of those days, huh?"

The fierce expression on Markev's face did not change, but he nodded ever so slightly and then charged once more. Adan considered different offensive and defensive options as his raging assistant barreled headlong at him and settled on an atypical choice. He feigned an initial parry and then allowed the man to land the vast majority of his subsequent blows. It hurt like hell, but Adan was self-aware enough to recognize his assistant's anger was justified. He wasn't seeking absolution, but he was willing to bet that giving Markev a chance to vent his anger would make him more amenable to the discussion that needed to come next.

The initial blows ended with Adan absorbing a fist to the face that dropped him to the deck in a heap. Instead of continuing the punishment, Markev stepped back and bounced on his toes as he waited for Adan to rise. After almost a minute of waiting for the bright spots to fade from his vision, Adan stood and stretched his neck out with a loud crack. He then mirrored Markev by bouncing on his toes.

"I'm sorry I didn't share the full plan with you, Markev."

"If I had known in advance, Adan, I would've returned to Earth to suffer their fate rather than have that blood on my hands. It's clear there's no sense arguing the morality of nuking the planet with you, but it was still an objectively stupid action."

"Fair point. Why stupid?"

Markev shook his head and moved towards the center of the circle. The battle was back on. Adan moved in as well, and the two once again traded punches and kicks. Having taken a reasonable beating to start things off, Adan focused on keeping the remainder of the fight even. It took significant exertion on his part as Markev was pushing hard, but the man's initial rage had boiled off as hoped. Adan finally connected a kick that made the giant drop to a knee for a moment, and he backed off to let Markev recover.

Adan posed his question again. "Why stupid?"

Markev replied as he stood. "You've given the Chancellor a wedge. It would have been one thing to fire those missiles when you and she had a unified message around the reason for doing so, but then you had to go blathering on about old-world explorers. Whether you meant to or not, you now own one hundred percent of that decision in the eyes of everyone on board. Our engineers should be fine either way because they trust you, but she can use this action to turn all of her people who don't share that trust against you if she chooses. There's a lot more of them right now than there are of us. We're smarter and we control the ship, but those are impossible odds."

Adan laughed and Markev looked at him with a quizzical expression. Instead of explaining, Adan charged and re-engaged the fisticuffs. After an extended period of fighting where equal punishment was absorbed by both of them, Adan attempted to smash Markev in the face. As his fist sailed toward its target, his bodyguard's knee rose up and slammed into his crotch. Even with the protective padding, the blow was delivered with such force that Adan collapsed to the deck like he'd been shot. His own punch glanced off Markev's face at the last instant but still carried enough force that it left the giant wobbling. He took a knee next to Adan and after a few moments spoke.

"What were you laughing about?"

It was another few seconds before Adan was capable of speech. "You're always better thinking through the interpersonal stuff than I am, and once again that's true. The Chancellor is looking to use that wedge before we've even left Earth. I met her yesterday, and she shared her concerns about unrest among the general population. She proposed that she remain the head of state and have final decision-making power.

She was nice enough to leave me in charge of the ship and the crew."

"Wow—she's moved a lot faster than I would have imagined."

"That was my thought as well, Markev. And it gets worse. She also shared how she's been hearing *rumors* about weapons caches that were smuggled onboard. She *really* hates the thought of an armed insurrection."

"Why do you think she's doing this right now, sir?"

"I'm not certain, but I suspect it's because she wants us to chart a different course than we agreed to. I don't know why it might be so much better that she wants to start this power grab now."

Markev was quiet for a moment before speaking. "We may be stuck, sir. Based on what you're saying, I'm guessing she's going to pull the trigger before we leave the system. We've got a lot of ex-military onboard who I planned to put in place to handle anything like this, but they're all still in cryostorage. It's impossible to get them thawed out and spun up that fast. We've got far better weapons than anything she could have snuck onto the ship, but on sheer numbers alone we're likely to lose."

They sat in silence for a few minutes as if they were chewing through various possible solutions on their own. Adan already knew what the answer was, but he wanted to give the illusion it was a last ditch, desperate idea rather than a long-considered plan. Finally, he stood and spoke tentatively.

"There's only one thing I can think of. I'm guessing you'll think it's just as bad an idea as me destroying Earth, but we may not have any other choice."

Adan extended a hand to Markev and helped him clamber up off the deck. Once he was standing, his bodyguard gestured for Adan to continue.

"What if we used the fire suppression system offensively?"

"Huh? How are we going to stop armed mutineers with water mist?"

"I'm not talking about the sprinklers, Markev. Those are only in place to deal with a localized blaze. What would we do if there was ever a huge fire that put the very survival of the asteroid at risk?"

His eyes went wide as Markev grasped what Adan was talking about. "You're suggesting we vent the ship?"

"I don't see what choice we have. Everything required can be done from the Bridge. We'll make sure all of our staff have reasons to be within our critical workspaces and then configure the venting protocol to protect those compartments. If we're right and the Chancellor follows through on this stunt, she'll get the surprise of her life. We'll maximize air pressure throughout the ship, override the safety systems on the interior hatches so they can't be closed, and then open all of the exterior hatches. Even if they all don't get swept out into the vacuum, whoever is left behind will die from the lack of atmosphere."

Markev gasped. "How did you become capable of so much killing, sir? It's bad enough to dispatch the East the way you did, but these are our own people. This feels like far, far too blunt of an instrument."

It took all of his dwindling patience for Adan to not snap at Markev. The man had been a trusted ally for so many years, so the frustration was that much greater when his support wasn't forthcoming at a time when Adan needed it most. If it had been anyone else Adan might have suspected some form of collusion with the Chancellor, but that was impossible for Markev. Well, he certainly hoped it was impossible.

"I'll say it again, Markev. What choice do we have? We can't let the Chancellor take over. Let's say I accepted her offer and retained nominal control of the ship and crew. You know that would only delay the inevitable. I guarantee she and I will butt heads about something where I can't compromise, and she'll figure out a way to get rid of me. We've worked too hard for too long. The survival of the species is at stake. We can't allow her to take over and screw everything up. You know the mission will fail with her in charge. Yes, it's a lot of people, but they aren't *our* people. They're *her* people. Our people are all in cryostorage. This action is drastic, but it will mean our people will wake up in a much healthier society—especially if we use the opportunity to build out the type of meritocratic structure you and I have always talked about."

Markev looked away as he considered the suggestion. He started to speak a couple of times but stopped. Finally, he responded.

"I can't get past the fact it's another five hundred thousand deaths, Adan. I don't want to allow Earth's twisted politics to take root up here either, but there has to be a better way to do it. Not every single one of the Chancellor's people can be horrible, can they?"

"We have no way of knowing. I can only imagine what kind of commitments they were forced to make to the Chancellor to secure their spots for the journey. There must have been an awful lot of dirty deals being struck back when they thought so few people were going to escape the planet."

Markev stared down at the deck in silence until he replied. "I will never forgive myself for it, but if we're forced to react in self-defense then I can support your plan. What are you thinking we do next?"

Adan wasn't sure yet, so he remained quiet as he paced back and forth. Markev used the time to start removing his pads. Adan was thrilled his bodyguard was done for the day since the session had served its purpose. If Adan had to worry about being dragged into a conflict with the Chancellor, he couldn't afford to be in any more pain than he already anticipated based on the beating he had absorbed. The various scenarios churned through his head for a few more minutes and then he spoke.

"I think we should provide her with the perfect opportunity to show her hand. If she's going to pull this off before we leave Earth, it means she's only got forty-eight hours. I'll wait until the end of the day today and then tell her we're running a series of drills tomorrow that will keep all of the engineers busy. This will ensure all of them are on duty and safe in the compartments we'll exclude from the venting. At the end of the conversation, I'll let her know I'm rejecting her leadership plan. She'll see that having all of the engineers concentrated in a small number of compartments will make taking over a lot easier. She's also going to think she'll be surprising us when we'll be busy and our attention will be elsewhere."

Markev grimaced as he spoke. "Impressive plan, Adan. I'm horrified at what we're about to do, but I agree we have no other choice."

With his mission accomplished, Adan turned to leave the compartment. "See you tomorrow, Markev. It will be the day we save the human race for all time."

CHAPTER TWENTY-ONE

The time for our journey is almost upon us.

Adan woke the next morning sore all over and took a few extra minutes to get out of bed. The pain meds he took prior to sleeping had worn off, so he reached for the container and dry swallowed two more. One got caught in his windpipe and triggered a cough which only served to make his suffering worse. Markev had really done some damage, but it was a fair trade for Adan given how the session allowed him to get his valued lieutenant aligned with his plans.

He shuffled to his private shower and stood under the hot water until it combined with the medication to take the edge off his aches. Once dry, he dressed gingerly without any pain until he had to bend over to adjust a shoe. Burning agony flared across his back, and he winced at the disappointment of undoing the relative comfort he had experienced after the extra-long shower.

As Adan went to leave, he paused at the hatch for one last look around his quarters. He had lived in the cabin throughout the building of the ship, and it was quite spacious as befit his position. His was one of the few cabins with such expansive views out to the stars, and Adan had spent hours gazing into the void envisioning how their mission might unfold. He hadn't ever considered a version of the journey where he would never see the spaceship's first jump away from Earth, but that was the situation he faced. He expected to return to the cabin at the end of the day, but there was a real chance he might never see it again if their plan failed. His conversation with the Chancellor prior to bed had confirmed his suspicions, and he expected she would act on her insurrection.

It's disappointing you won't take me up on my offer, Adan, but not surprising. I assume hearing how the unrest has spiked much higher in the day since we last spoke won't change anything, but I'd feel remiss if I didn't share that fact with you and give you one last chance to reconsider. Good luck with your drills tomorrow. I'll use the time to see if I can figure out a way we might be able to keep all of these people happy.

Of course, the Chancellor had not said anything explicit, but Adan recognized the threat as he read between the lines. Markev had reluctantly agreed with that assessment, and they had reconfirmed their plan.

They would not move preemptively, but if the Chancellor left them no choice then Adan was prepared to definitively end the conflict. If killing half a million of her followers was the price to protect the future of humanity, he would pay it. They expected the venting protocol to work, but for obvious reasons had never performed a widespread test. If it failed, they would be trapped like rats.

Adan skipped the transport system in favor of walking to the bridge so he could loosen his aching muscles. Markev was present and nodded at Adan as he entered. The bodyguard approached and then spoke softly once he was close.

"Sir—everything is ready as we discussed. I have configured the venting protocol to open the entire ship except for those compartments where our crew is working. Everyone is in place for the drill and awaiting your final orders."

"Thank you, Markev. Please set me up for an announcement to everyone."

A few seconds later Markev nodded to signal they were ready to broadcast.

"Good morning. The time for our journey is almost upon us. Today marks our final preparations, and tomorrow we say farewell to our solar system. The next twenty-four hours will begin the future of the human race, and everyone among the crew is prepared to do whatever it takes to ensure its survival. That is all."

The Chancellor wasn't the only one who could deliver messages laden with alternate meaning. Would it make any difference if she was moving down the path Adan suspected? Almost certainly not. On the off chance it might give an influential lieutenant of hers pause, though, it was worth a try.

The next few hours passed without incident. The crew operated just as Adan had trained them. Drill after drill was executed with flawless results. His people were ready to do their jobs, and he could not possibly have been any prouder. Just as Adan was getting lulled into believing that perhaps he and Markev had misread the situation, the communications coordinator spoke.

"Sir—a group of the Chancellor's top advisors are requesting entrance to Engineering Control. They would like to observe the remainder of our drills from there."

Markev stood across the compartment. His aide nodded to Adan in acknowledgment that he shared the same thought—it was beginning. A light flashed on the armrest of Adan's chair to signify an incoming private communication. He accepted it and was greeted by the Chancellor.

"Good afternoon, Adan. I trust the drills are proceeding as expected. There are some of my people who I would love to have observe in a few of the compartments. I know how well you've trained your team, and I think it would be inspiring for the rest of us to witness such a smooth-running operation firsthand.

I'd like to bring a few people with me and come watch from the bridge myself if you are OK with that."

"Good day, Madam Chancellor. Thanks for your interest in observing. We're at a critical point right now, so this very moment isn't the best time. I'll be happy to have your people observe, but I ask they wait a few more hours until we've completed our core operational drills. I hope you understand, but I just don't want to subject my crew to any distractions right now."

There was an extended silence. Adan envisioned the Chancellor having muted her communicator as she consulted with her Chief of Staff before she spoke.

"That's understandable, Adan, but surprising. I would have thought you'd be thrilled to show off what a finely-honed machine you're running here. Are you sure I can't get you to change your mind?"

"Quite sure, Madam Chancellor. I'm not saying no, I'm just saying not right now. I'll update you in ninety minutes."

Adan cut the connection without waiting for a response and spoke to Comms. "Inform all section chiefs that none of the Chancellor's people should be allowed to disrupt our drills by entering any compartment until they hear otherwise from me. Is that clear?"

The man nodded and Adan rose from his chair. In doing so, he noticed he was stiffening up and the pain was returning. Additional meds beckoned, but carried the risk of dulling his senses or thought processes. Instead, he took the time to stretch and knead his sorest muscles until Markev cleared his throat. His lieutenant gestured him over and Adan approached.

The video monitor in front of Markev cycled through various security feeds from around the spaceship. In almost all of them, there were groups of three to five people who walked together. The fact there were people moving about was not a surprise, but Adan picked up on the same clues Markev must have. All of the groups were not only walking with a purpose, but the individuals appeared to move with the stolid, confident gait of those who had experienced military training. Furthermore, many of the people were carrying bags or cases which were large enough to conceal one or more weapons. He shook his head as he spoke.

"Dammit—she's making her move. Get the countermeasures finalized and give me a communication channel to all of the compartments where the crew is working."

Adan paused and then spoke when Markev pointed at him. "Attention, crew. I have unfortunate news to report. The Chancellor has taken it upon herself to lead a mutiny against all of us. This is not a drill. I repeat, this is not a drill. As you might imagine, I refuse to allow the Chancellor to succeed as we've all worked too hard to let some politician ruin everything. We have a plan to neutralize her forces, though I hope such drastic measures will not be necessary. Until you hear otherwise, remain at your stations and do not allow anyone to enter your compartments. It's critical for your safety that all hatches remain secured until I give you the all clear."

Once the connection was cut Adan turned back to Markev. "Get me the Chancellor and put her up on the main display."

After a few minutes of waiting the large screen at the front of the compartment lit up with a close-up of the Chancellor's face. The size of the image exaggerated the woman's age by making her numerous wrinkles look like deep valleys and fissures. She smiled and spoke.

"Hello, Adan. To what do I owe this honor? I thought you were going to be too busy with your drills for a while longer."

"Ma'am—you can cut the crap. We see what you're doing."

"Whatever are you talking about, Adan?" The Chancellor paused for a moment and then shook her head. "No—forget it. I had thought I wanted to play around with you for a while, but my heart isn't in it. You're right—we're taking over. You can let it happen the easy way and save your crew, or you can cause a lot of innocent people to get killed. Either way, you're never leaving Earth. You and Markev are going to remain behind in orbit, though without spacesuits you won't have very long to ponder the view."

"You sound awfully confident, Madam Chancellor, for a woman who has a handful of people running around with some light weapons."

The Chancellor laughed. "That's what you've seen so far, Adan, but what gives me so much confidence is what you haven't. It's not a handful of people but instead fifty thousand. And while some are indeed only carrying light weapons, far larger numbers will be shortly geared up with battle armor and a full combat load."

Adan's engineers were trying to remain calm around the compartment, but their fear was palpable. They weren't soldiers and wanted no part of violent conflict. He wanted to reassure them everything would be fine, but he needed to deal with the Chancellor first. She continued to speak.

"You've got us locked out now, Adan, but you know you can't hold out for long. Don't force me to pull out the laser drills and carve all of you from those compartments. Save your crew. This can be your parting gift to the human race. You rescued all of us by building this ark, and now you can allow us to leave this dead world behind. Open the compartments and let my staff take over. You have my word no one other than you and the bodyguard will get hurt."

"Wow, ma'am. I suspected this would happen eventually, but you surprised me by making your move so quickly. I'm sorry it has come to this. I guess you've left me no choice. I'll open all of the hatches for you now."

Adan signaled Markev to commence the plan. The woman up on the screen appeared smug and satisfied with what she must have thought was a decisive and bloodless victory. Then the high-pressure warning sirens began to wail, and panic washed over her face. A few heartbeats later she disappeared from the camera's view with nothing but a fading scream as the exterior and interior hatches across the spaceship were opened to the vacuum of space and the explosive decompression sucked her and all of her followers out into the void. She had ruled a billion people during her life, but in death she was just one of five hundred thousand new satellites that began their slow orbit around the dead homeworld below.

CHAPTER TWENTY-TWO

Those days are over.

During their first month after departing Earth, Adan set a demanding pace for his team that included three FTL jumps per day. In theory, the spaceship had enough automation it could be operated for an extended period by a single knowledgeable individual. Optimal crew size, however, was well above the thousand engineers who were the only people conscious after the purge of the Chancellor and her cronies. Without their assistance for those activities that didn't require special skills, Adan's crew was forced to shoulder the full burden of maintaining operations.

The stress showed on everyone, not least Adan himself. Even though he was often exhausted, he was unable to get restorative sleep during his limited downtime. Instead, he usually tossed in his bed restlessly as his mind refused to stop spinning. He had convinced himself that he was doing a sufficient job of coping until Markev had commented a few days earlier that Adan's short temper was emerging again.

With the time overdue for planning the first wave of reinforcements to revive from cryostorage, Adan called his section leaders together to identify the most urgent profiles to start thawing out. He was the last to arrive for the meeting, and he found everyone talking quietly. The group's discussion struck him as being almost furtive since it halted when he walked through the hatch. Adan wanted to believe nothing was amiss given how Markev was present, but a low-level anxiety gnawed at him nonetheless. He called the group to order and spoke once everyone was sitting around the table except Markev. His bodyguard remained standing as he often preferred to do.

"I asked Logistics to distribute their draft plan before the meeting. I trust you all received it and have had a chance to review. Any questions?"

The woman who was in charge of the flight hangar raised her hand. Adan acknowledged her with a nod.

"Sir—I looked at the plan, and I have to say I'm pretty surprised by the slow personnel ramp-up it describes. As far as I understand, we've got capacity for ten million people to be awake and the ideal crew size is at least fifty thousand. If I'm understanding the plan, we'll still only have a couple of thousand people thawed out after a few months. Why such a slow pace?"

"It's a great question about a topic I've given a lot of thought to. While I want to relieve the worst of the strain on our teams by providing additional staffing, I believe we must take our time and be mindful of the society we create on this ship."

Adan checked his audience and recognized how most people appeared skeptical. He stood and continued his explanation.

"Everyone who is awake right now is the very best at what they do. For too long, those of us who have tremendous knowledge and ability were subject to the whims of politicians back on Earth. They either ruled based on how it benefited their own fortunes or chose whatever lowest common denominator policy would get them enough support to maintain the largest base of power. Those days are over."

The ability to engineer the society of his dreams was always a benefit Adan expected to come out of his spaceship project, but he had assumed it wouldn't happen until much later in the journey. The Chancellor's sooner-than-expected removal provided an opportunity to accelerate his timeline, and he was determined to not let it pass by. Many people leaned forward in their seats, clearly intrigued by what Adan was saying. It was time to sell his vision.

"The politician class is gone, so we should allow all of their old leadership structures to fade away with them. Democracy as practiced by them was a farce. An occasional vote by the people was tolerated to provide an illusion of participation in government. All while the gears of power kept grinding and chewing up the people doing the real work and creating the real value. This was done for the benefit of a very few who had never earned it except by nature of having learned how the political game was played. We are better than that and we can do better than that.

"Our future lies in a system driven by meritocracy instead of democracy. Democracy was government by the many, but meritocracy will be government by the best. Isn't that what we all want? We're the most technologically advanced society humanity has ever created. We shouldn't give leadership to the strongest or the wiliest but instead to those who are demonstrably, measurably the best. We can build a system like this, but it needs to start from the ground up and be slowly nurtured. I directed Logistics to develop a plan specifically with this in mind. We'll take the time necessary for this group to solidify our new society and, only then, introduce new people to it over time. As we scale up we can add people faster and faster, but in the early stages it will be important we keep the pace slow to build the strongest foundation possible."

"Sir?"

It was the man who ran communications. Adan found him to be impossibly annoying more often than not, but he was superb at what he did so therefore tolerated. He gestured for the man to speak.

"I appreciate how you believe we're all the best, but I know for a fact there are people in cryostorage who are better at their jobs than some of the people around this table right now. Why should all of us get to be in charge just because we're awake first?"

"Great question, Comms. My intent is not to say this group will run the spaceship forever. I'm saying instead that we need to develop a system whereby we can be certain the best have an opportunity to rise to the top and earn their place among the leadership. You may be right that someone in cryostorage right now is better than you or one of your peers. The system I want to build will only be a success if it allows those people to be recognized and rise above any inferior competition. True, objective meritocracy."

There were now a lot of nodding heads around the compartment, and it was clear Adan's message was resonating with most. Comms raised his hand again, and Adan acknowledged him once more.

"What about your position atop the hierarchy, sir? Will you allow your new meritocracy to surface someone who might be objectively better suited to have final decision-making authority than you?"

Adan smiled. "This interchange is a perfect example of why I love working with great engineers— you're rarely shy about asking tough questions. Our new society will work best if we all become comfortable with that level of candor. Sounds like there might be something more underpinning your inquiry. Would you like to expand on your line of thinking to better allow me and your peers to understand your perspective?"

The man made eye contact with a few other members of the flight operations staff who each nodded at him before he spoke. "Well, there are a number of us who are conflicted about following a man who was willing to commit genocide to bolster the resolve of the people onboard this ship. Sir."

Adan almost remained calm in the face of the man's question. Though his pulse quickened at the word *genocide,* a couple of deep breaths brought it back towards normal. Then the man's mouth formed the slightest hint of a smirk, and Adan reacted as his gut had initially demanded. He charged at Comms and in one motion lifted him out of his chair and slammed him against the nearest bulkhead. The man weighed no more than fifty kilos soaking wet and must never have done a moment of physical training.

Adan jumped on top of Comms as the man slumped to the floor and rained down blow after blow with his fists. Within seconds, he was yanked off the deck and wrapped in a bear hug by Markev. Adan struggled against his aide's viselike grip for a few seconds until he calmed enough for the immediate rage to dissipate. Markev must have sensed the shift because he loosened his hold although he didn't release Adan. A couple of his peers helped Comms off the deck and guided him out of the compartment. Once the hatch shut behind them, Markev released his hold. Adan stood up and straightened his uniform which had become disheveled in the struggle. He turned to Markev.

"Review the rest of the plan and discuss implementation timelines with those who remain."

Without another word, Adan strode out of the hatch and left tumult behind as people showered Markev with questions and concerns.

CHAPTER TWENTY-THREE

Let's just get it out there.

Adan's fist crashed into Markev's head and sent his bodyguard sprawling to the deck. Adan scrambled to stomp on the giant's belly, but the man rolled away from the blow at the last second and then grabbed Adan's ankle and threw him off balance. While Adan regained his footing, Markev popped up off the deck and turned to him and spoke.

"It's been twenty-four hours since you attacked Comms. I was tempted to cancel our sparring session, but I was hoping you might have calmed down by now. I can see that I was wrong."

Adan didn't respond but instead charged at Markev and pounded him with a flurry of kicks interspersed with punches to the man's core. Markev was able to block most of the blows, but enough landed with sufficient force to once again send him crashing to the deck. Adan backed off and downed a big slug from his water container while allowing his aide an opportunity to recover. Markev didn't stand right away, but instead spoke from his knees.

"You're not yourself. Do you see that? The rest of us do."

"What the hell are you talking about, Markev?"

"You haven't been the same man who hired me for a couple of years now. You've always been a demanding boss, but you've started to behave more like a sociopath. Even before what happened yesterday, I can think of another half-dozen situations where your response to someone who challenged you was entirely non-proportional and inappropriate. I had assumed it was all of the stress catching up to you, but your reaction yesterday was something else. It was pure, unmitigated rage. That isn't anything I've seen from you before, and it was scary."

Adan wanted to spar more, but Markev clearly had something to get off his chest. He sat down and leaned against the bulkhead while he took another long swallow from his container before he replied.

"I tried not to react yesterday. I swear I did. I was excited to share our vision with everyone, and at first it was going so well. And then that little skinny punk started talking about genocide, and I just had to wipe his stupid smirk off his face."

Markev shook his head. "That's what I'm talking about, Adan. Three years ago you would have gutted someone who talked to you like that, but you would have done it with words. You would have torn him apart with a logical argument and left him quivering and useless. That ability is why I and so many others chose to follow you. What you've done recently instead is shut down dissent by force. Whether it's that woman you kicked off the asteroid a while back, or beating the crap out of Comms, you just can't seem to tolerate any semblance of disagreement. What do you think might be going on?"

"Stop beating around the bush, Markev. I'm pretty sure you've got a theory. Let's just get it out there."

"I'm certain the changes started back when we were testing the faster-than-light technology. Your temper started to flare far more than it had before. I know I was feeling incredible stress too at the time, and it was interesting because as soon as I stopped doing as much flying things got better. You, however, kept the same pace of FTL jumps almost until the end. Your behavior returned to normal once the test flights tapered off, but then everything flared up again with you once we left Earth and started jumping so much."

Adan didn't agree with Markev. He remembered profound exhaustion from that time when the flight testing was going on, but he just couldn't see how his behavior had changed enough to warrant suspicion something untoward had happened due to the FTL technology. Regardless, he owed his longtime aide at least the consideration of hearing him out.

"What's the solution you propose, Markev?"

"Two things, sir. First—let's slow down the pace of jumps. You're not the only one behaving like you're negatively affected right now, but let's be sure we don't trigger similarly severe symptoms in anyone else. Second—you should temporarily transfer final authority to a small council and take a break from any responsibility."

"Now I'm dealing with my second coup in our first month? And led by you no less?"

Adan had tried to project lightheartedness with his response as it was *mostly* a joke, but from the look on Markev's face it had not landed as desired. His heart had skipped a beat when he processed the man's suggestion about Adan taking a break. It was likely whatever buried emotion had caused that physical reaction had also imparted a different tone to his voice than intended. He rushed to defuse the situation by cutting their discussion short.

"I don't think you're right about the FTL, Markev, but I'll look at easing off the pace a little. I definitely don't agree there's any problem that warrants action as drastic as me transferring my authority, though. I promise you I'll give it some careful thought, but I need to get going right now."

Adan stood and walked out of the training dojo. He made it thirty paces down the passageway before noticing he still wore his fighting pads. He paused for a moment and considered going back but kept moving rather than risk facing Markev again.

Why was he experiencing such a strong negative reaction to his aide's suggestion? They had worked together for so long that Markev was the only human alive in whom he had as much faith as himself. If the man was worried about him, Adan should simply assume the concern was genuine and trust there was nothing harbored but good intentions. Something darker nagged at him though.

Markev had not been happy with many of Adan's choices during the building of the spaceship. He was always dutiful and accepted the outcome in the end after listening to Adan's viewpoints, but it had been clear on multiple occasions he had strong feelings in opposition. Adan knew himself well enough to understand that if he was constantly faced with conclusions he believed were wrong that eventually he would take matters into his own hands. Why should Markev be any different? He was a brilliant individual who might have been as successful as Adan if he had chosen a different path earlier in his life. Wouldn't someone like that grow tired of repeatedly having to accept and defend decisions he felt were wrong?

Then there was the matter of Adan's gut. Months had been spent prior to their departure working through the game theory around the situation with the Chancellor. All of that careful analysis had concluded there was no way she would attempt to take over the ship until much later in their journey. Adan's gut then latched on to her words and tone and in a matter of days overruled his earlier conclusion. His intuition had undeniably been a major source of his success through the years, and his ability to read the Chancellor was just another example of its power. If he was experiencing some form of gut response suggesting there was hidden subtext to Markev's words, shouldn't he trust that more than the man himself?

He didn't want to believe his aide might be working in opposition to him, but Adan knew enough to understand that bias was all the more reason why he had to give it such careful consideration. Where he got stuck was what to do if it was true. How could Adan hold sway over the rest of the crew if he couldn't manage to maintain the loyalty of his longtime lieutenant? He didn't have an answer, but it was clear to him that making any move against Markev would likely doom his ability to ever control anyone else among the current crew.

There had to be a way out, but every path Adan considered ended somewhere he wasn't prepared to contemplate. As he reached his cabin, Adan promised himself to get some rest and then attack the problem with a fresh perspective in the morning. He stripped out of his gear, jumped into his bunk, and stared at the ceiling as his thoughts instead swirled even faster.

CHAPTER TWENTY-FOUR

It's the only way.

Five hours later Adan had still not had a moment's sleep. He had chased every possible solution to its logical conclusion, and every single option ended the same way. If Markev or the rest of the crew took any action that removed Adan from command, it would absolutely be the end of humanity. There was no one else who could step up and lead the mission to success like he could. Only Adan could ensure the survival of the species, and he convinced himself it was time to take decisive action and ensure no one got in his way. The only question that remained was whether Markev would support his conclusion, and there was only one way to get an accurate answer.

Adan walked to his shower and adjusted the water's temperature to the coldest setting he could tolerate without having his teeth chatter. He stood under its icy blast until he had shocked every cell in his body into full alert. He got out and dried off, but his shivering didn't stop until he was dressed and had done five minutes of calisthenics to get his blood flowing again. He walked briskly to the bridge to find a skeleton crew on duty as expected. Comms was in charge during third shift, and he greeted Adan warily before turning back to his workstation.

Adan sat in his command chair and accessed his control panel. He knew what configuration changes were needed and he made them quickly. Just as he completed his work, the light flashed for an incoming private communication. Markev. Adan accepted the request.

"What going on, Adan?"

"What's wrong with me waking up early and deciding to visit the bridge?"

"Adan—I can't have you in there while you're in such a questionable mental state. I've instructed Comms and the rest of the crew there to restrain you until I arrive. I'll escort you to your quarters and we can talk this out."

When Adan looked up from his screen he discovered the bridge crew had arrayed themselves in a semicircle in front of his chair. They all appeared nervous except for Comms. The skinny engineer bounced with excitement at the prospect Adan might resist and he'd get to pile on with some retribution. Adan replied to Markev.

"I'm sorry, but that plan isn't going to work for me."

Before anyone could react, Adan reached to the small of his back and extracted the mini blaster he had confiscated from Jania. He had subsequently spent time training with it at the range and had come to appreciate its perfect balance and light weight. With six quick pulls of the trigger, Adan delivered a center mass kill shot into each of the crew. They all collapsed to the deck and were dead before the first blast echo faded away. He turned back to Markev. The color had drained from his aide's face.

"What have you done...?"

"It's not what I've done, it's what I'm about to do."

"You can't do this, Adan. You can't."

"It's the only way. You know that. We need a clean break from everything that brought us to this point. We'll build a new society, one person at a time. That society can be everything we want it to be. We'll start slow and only add more people as we're certain all of our precepts are taking hold. This is how we'll save the human race, Markev. We've got to become better than we were and that requires a fresh start."

"You keep killing people, Adan, in the name of saving the species. At what point does it become clear you're just trying to enact your own personal vision for it at any price?"

"Markev—don't be like this. I know you believe in my vision even if you don't wholeheartedly agree with the methods I might have used along the way to see it realized. Stay by my side. Help me build a society that will thrive for a billion years across the universe."

Markev was silent and Adan started to get excited at the prospect he had kept his aide in the fold. Then, the man spoke.

"If I ever see you again, I will kill you with my bare hands. To save the species."

Adan was crestfallen but knew fast action remained imperative. He kept his eyes focused on his bodyguard while his fingers manipulated the control panel and added one final compartment to the venting protocol—Markev's quarters.

"I'm sorry it's ending this way, Markev. Thank you for all you've done for me through the years."

Before the man on the other end of the screen could say another word, Adan keyed the code to once again purge the ship. The pressure alarm wailed, but Markev did not disappear from view the same way the Chancellor had. Loose items from his quarters flew past the camera's view, but Markev remained firmly in his seat. He was in obvious distress, but managed to keep his eyes focused on Adan's as he held his breath.

Adan didn't understand how his aide avoided getting ejected into space, but he knew he couldn't bear to watch the man die. Instead, he closed his eyes and focused on deep, regular breathing.

Adan woke with a start. He assumed he must have dozed off for only a moment, but the video monitor revealed the truth. Markev was long dead. A trickle of blood had escaped the corner of his mouth and frozen solid. Adan's console showed he had slept for almost ten hours. His body screamed for more rest, but he forced himself to stay awake. He needed to put the final cleanup behind him before sleeping again.

The biggest consequence of Adan dozing off was that all of the external airlocks and internal hatches had remained open and exposed the entire ship to the deathly cold of space for an extended period of time. There wouldn't be any damage as a result and he flooded it with atmosphere to restore pressure, but those parts of the structure closest to exterior hatches would remain impossibly cold. Fortunately, there was an airlock near the bridge which had a cabinet stocked with emergency pressure suits that would protect him from the chill.

Once he had closed the hatches around the asteroid and there was sufficient atmosphere outside of the bridge, Adan opened the hatch only to have his body recoil from the cold. He dashed for the airlock and returned to the warmth of the bridge to don the suit. He didn't want to put on the helmet, but the painful cold he had just sampled so quickly proved the deciding factor.

Adan spent the next thirty minutes lugging the six corpses of the bridge crew into the airlock. Most were like Comms in being fairly light and easy to transport, but a couple were fairly sizable and needed to be dragged rather than carried. Once they were all inside, he sealed the inner hatch and then opened the external one to send the six to join the rest of their fellow crew out in the vacuum.

A few minutes later Adan arrived at Markev's quarters and discovered why the man had not been sucked out into the void. He must have expected Adan's action because he had used a cord to secure himself to his chair which was attached to the deck. Adan used the utility blade attached to his suit to cut the cord and released his aide's corpse from the seat.

Unlike the bodies in the bridge, Markev had been exposed to icy temperatures while Adan had slept. His quarters were a scant few meters from one of the exterior airlocks, so he was partially frozen and more unwieldy as a result. When the state of the body was combined with the man's sizable mass and Adan's deepening exhaustion, it took all of Adan's strength to move the corpse. He was surprised to find Markev wearing a bracelet he had never noticed before, but it had proven useful as it was firmly attached and helped Adan maintain a stronger grasp around the hulking man's wrist.

After struggling with the body, Adan manhandled Markev into the nearby airlock. He knelt down and forced the man's eyes closed before letting his hand linger on his bodyguard's face for a few moments. It shouldn't have ended like this, but he was convinced he was doing the right thing if his mission to save the human race was to be successful. Tears pooled in his eyes, so Adan rushed to get things over with before he became emotional. Thirty seconds later, the exterior hatch was opened, and Markev was sucked out to rest forever among the stars.

Adan struggled back to his quarters and was reduced to shuffling his feet over the last few hundred meters. He knew all of the systems were fine, but it was almost like the artificial gravity had been damaged since his body required an effort to move like it was twice as heavy. He closed the hatch behind him and stripped out of the pressure suit. Even though his cabin remained warm as it had not been exposed to the vacuum and the pressure suit should have protected him from the cold throughout the rest of the ship, he shivered uncontrollably. He stumbled into the bathing area for his second shower of the day, though for this one he cranked the temperature to just short of scalding.

Once the shaking stopped, Adan turned the water off and stepped out of the shower. He skipped the towel and instead stumbled straight to his bunk. Without another thought, he sprawled across his bed and fell unconscious within seconds.

CHAPTER TWENTY-FIVE

This whole journey is a massive waste of time!

"Wow."

Zax said the word quietly, under his breath, as soon as Mase stopped projecting the contents of the log file. They were sitting together in a small conference room that Mase had access to based on being a senior pilot. The man grinned at Zax as he spoke.

"That's as far as I've gone. Pretty amazing stuff, right?"

Amazing struck Zax as a wild understatement. His head swam under the deluge of information he had just learned.

Earth was dead.

Billions of humans had died along with their homeworld.

All of the horror was unleashed by the Ship's builder.

That same builder had murdered the original Crew.

Mase continued. "This invalidates everything we've ever been told. Earth's climate didn't collapse. This Adan guy destroyed it. We aren't descended from the brightest and most talented people from Earth. Everyone in that first Crew was killed by Adan. Our entire history is a lie."

Zax remained speechless as he struggled to fit all of the pieces together. Mase was right about how the news upended what everyone onboard had long understood, but that paled in comparison to what struck Zax as one piece of hugely valuable new knowledge. Knowledge with immediate impact.

"If Earth's definitively dead, then we *must* stop heading there. This whole journey is a massive waste of time! Even if we continue onwards for some stupid reason, all of these preparations for a final showdown with the other humans should be halted because we're not going to find them there. Why would anyone be defending a planet that was so utterly slagged?"

Mase stared at him wordlessly. It was all so logical and clear to Zax, yet Mase continued to look at him blankly. There was another huge benefit to the news as far as Zax was concerned, and he couldn't help but grin as he delved into it.

"We'll be heroes for bringing this to the attention of the Flight Boss. This isn't as big a deal as when I saved his life back during the Revolution, but it has to be at least valuable enough for me to get back into the Crew. Right?"

Mase's mouth hung agape for a few long beats until he replied. "I can see why it's important we get the news out there about Earth somehow. But are you saying you want to tell the Boss I've been hacking the Ship's AIs?"

"Of course not. We'll figure out a story as to why you hacked into just this one."

Mase shook his head. "I'm sorry, Zax, but I just don't see how that makes any sense. If the Boss hears *anything* about hacking the AIs, we'll be lucky to only get Culled. I know you want to stay onboard and out of cryosleep, but this isn't the way to do it."

Zax was stunned. He was well aware Mase had his quirks, but would have guessed he'd be savvy enough to see the opportunity in front of them. Past experience proved there was always a risk in dealing with the Boss, but this situation appeared to provide nothing but upside. Zax did have far more to gain than Mase, so perhaps it made sense for him to bear all of the risk.

"I'll understand, Mase, if you don't want to get mixed up in this. I have too much to gain, though, and I'm not going to let an opportunity to get back into the Crew go by. How about we figure out a way for you to help me represent all of this as being my own doing? We'll keep your name out of it. Just like when I went to

Imair with the information you uncovered about the other humans."

Mase paused for a couple of secs before replying. "I think there has to be a better way, Zax, but I'll help you put together a story that doesn't expose my role in this."

"Thank you. What do you think about me sharing the information with Kalare first? Getting her to help present it to the Boss would make sure he pays attention and doesn't just dismiss it out of hand because it's coming from me."

Of course, Zax had an ulterior motive in wanting to enlist Kalare. Her participation in a situation where he was trying to support the Omega rather than undermine the man could only help to rebuild their friendship. Kalare would be thrilled to see him put aside his antipathy towards the Boss for the good of the Ship. Mase nodded.

"I think that's a good idea."

Zax stood and went to leave. "Great! I'm going to go see if I can find out when my Plug will be reactivated. Any story we come up with about me doing the hacking will be far more plausible if I accomplished it after I got Plugged In again."

"Hey—there's still more content in the log. Don't you think we should check out the rest?"

Zax couldn't envision anything they might learn that would be more valuable than what was already in their possession. The potential of restoring his relationship with Kalare and getting returned to the

Crew were both so attractive he was bouncing out of his seat with anticipation, and he wanted to figure out the timeline for next steps. However, tracking down the status of his Plug was primarily an excuse to feel like he was taking action rather than anything that was actually useful. He sat back down.

"You're right, Mase. Let's see what else is in here. I can't imagine anything would be more valuable, but maybe we'll be surprised."

CHAPTER TWENTY-SIX

I have unfortunate news to share with you all.

As Adan walked the passageway, he checked behind him for what must have been the hundredth time in the last ninety days. During most of that time he had known for certain he was the only conscious soul aboard the spaceship, but for some reason he had repeatedly experienced the most profound sense he was being watched.

Yet again he was surrounded by only deserted passageway, so Adan continued on his way. It was an important milestone, though, in being the first time it was actually possible someone else was nearby. After many prior iterations were halted and restarted, Adan had allowed the ship's primary Artificial Intelligence to run a cryostorage removal countdown all the way to zero.

It wasn't that Adan kept changing his mind when previous countdowns neared zero, but rather the stops and restarts were all part of his master plan. Ever since he woke up by himself on the asteroid, Adan had instructed the AI to run a continuous series of cryostorage countdowns as a safeguard against anything happening to him. The irony of Adan dying by accident after everything he had sacrificed and for that to then result in the only remnants of the species moldering in cryostorage for all eternity was far too much to ponder. The repeated countdowns acted as a dead man's switch and ensured the AI would waken a new crew if any misfortune were to befall Adan.

The AI had become a much-appreciated partner during the months Adan toiled nonstop on his own. Though his conversations with the system couldn't take the place of real human interaction, Adan appreciated its company and assistance. He had foregone non-critical operations and the asteroid hadn't done a single FTL jump since he purged the crew, but with the AI's help he had accomplished everything necessary to first identify and then receive the first wave of citizens for his newly designed version of human society.

Adan had never been more exhausted, but all of the labor had a pleasant side effect. The insomnia which had gripped him for the first thirty days of the ship's voyage had subsided during the subsequent ninety. He returned to his typical five hours per night within days of purging the crew. This meant he was asleep each night as soon as he closed his eyes and woke each morning feeling genuinely refreshed.

As he approached the compartment where the first fifty replacement crew awaited him, Adan found himself equal parts terrified and thrilled at the prospect of speaking with live humans. The group of fifty had been awakened a short time earlier and had been instructed to report directly to the meeting compartment where snacks had been left for them to stave off their bodies' craving for solid food. A side effect of coming out of cryostorage was the need to gorge like one of those extinct animals that used to hibernate all winter long—back when Earth experienced an actual winter, of course.

Adan entered the compartment and the conversations stopped. Those people who had gathered to stand around in small groups returned to their seats. Almost everyone had a pile of food in front of them from which they continued to eat as they waited for everyone to settle and for Adan to speak.

"Welcome back. For those who may not know me, my name is Adan and I'm the person responsible for the design and creation of this spaceship. I have unfortunate news to share with you all."

What had created Adan's terror around this moment was his worry about how this first batch of crew replacements would react to the cover story he had manufactured to explain the situation aboard the spaceship. He had done everything possible to doctor the AI's memory as well as the ship's public log files to support his fictional version of events, so he was confident it would stand up to investigation—particularly if he sold it convincingly up front. His introduction caught everyone's attention and almost all of them leaned forward in their seats. He continued.

"A few days ago, I was on a solo flight to evaluate a change to our scout shuttles. I played a key role in the development of our spacecraft and have continued to be the primary test pilot. I was almost three hundred thousand kilometers away when I received a short burst of comms traffic indicating the ship was encountering an unknown technical problem. I asked for clarification but got no reply. I returned immediately, but by the time I got back I found a horrific situation. The entirety of the ship had somehow been opened to space and everyone not in cryostorage was vented out. The five hundred thousand people who remained awake at launch plus another million who had been brought out of cryostorage in the years since were all gone and left behind in the ship's wake."

There were audible gasps around the room. A handful of people became overwhelmed with emotion and buried their faces in their hands. One young woman who was seated in the back row raised her hand and Adan acknowledged her. She spoke with a light accent he could not quite place.

"Sir—how long have we been asleep? How far are we from Earth?"

"You've all been in cryostorage for five years. Our course during that time involved an intentional redirection so we're far closer to our homeworld than you would expect based on that timeline. Our initial heading on departure from Earth was selected so we could evaluate two relatively nearby systems which we believed might have proven capable of supporting human life. To our dismay, both planets proved to be dead ends. After visiting the second system, we turned back the way we came because our analysis had shown that was a more likely direction in which to find a greater concentration of the Class M planets which will support life."

Most of the people in the room were hanging on Adan's every word. There weren't any outward signs among them that anyone was seeing through his various lies. The one exception was the woman who asked the questions. Something about her expression bothered Adan, but he put the worry aside as more hands shot up.

The next few questions involved clarifications about the accident and its effects. Adan used the opportunity to assure everyone he had identified the root cause and made the necessary changes to prevent it from happening again. Finally, a man in the front row asked the question Adan was most excited for.

"Why are we the people you've woken up first, sir?"

Adan smiled. "Thank you for the question as it leads into the last topic I wanted to cover. Out of the billion people in our hold, you've all been removed from cryosleep because you're among those who are the most intelligent and qualified to run this spaceship.

"I imagine that for all of you it feels like just yesterday you were back on Earth. If you were like me, you always chafed at the inefficiency of the world around you and how we allowed politicians who knew nothing about systems thinking to manage the biggest and most complex system of all—our society. In partnership with the Chancellor, we spent the last five years adapting the best parts of our old world to create an improved system of governance for our new home on this asteroid. She recognized as much as I did that new challenges would arise as we travel the universe on this rock to seek new worlds for our species. These challenges would require a new way of organizing and managing our society. We spent the first few years of our journey experimenting with different solutions until we came upon a version that had lasted for almost three years until the time of the accident."

Many heads nodded vigorously as expected. Having worked among brilliant engineers all his career, the thought processes of his audience were a known quantity and Adan knew how to reinforce their implicit biases. Acknowledging how the old system was broken and then talking about iterating across different possible ideas until an optimal solution was identified was designed to hit all of their logical pleasure centers. The body language around the room confirmed he was squarely on target and he continued.

"We created a true meritocracy. Rather than some form of representative government where less technically adept people sought power through the usage of rhetoric and force of personality, we instead focused on developing a society where every member's contributions and capabilities could be measured and scored. Those individuals who rose to the top by exhibiting valuable skills would have the greatest influence. If the people crewing this ship are the best of humanity, then power should rest with those who are objectively the best of the best.

"Later today I will introduce you to the Leaderboard. This is the system we developed to underpin this new meritocracy. It allows for the assessment of credits and demerits and tracks everyone's score so we always know precisely who among the crew is performing well versus who is not keeping up. Those who do the best will rise to the top of the asteroid's hierarchy while those who don't will be stuck with the more menial jobs."

A new hand shot up and an older woman spoke as soon as Adan nodded in her direction.

"Did you say before that you had grown this new society to over a million people, sir?"

Adan nodded in response. Of all the lies he told, this was the one that bothered him the most because it was unknown whether a true meritocracy was capable of scaling up to such large numbers. He was proud of the Leaderboard system and was convinced it would prove to be the most critical tool for managing a group of high-performing individuals, but it could just as easily fall apart as soon as they had more than a few thousand crew. The woman who asked the first question had her hand raised again, but Adan ended the meeting before she or anyone else could undermine its success.

"I understand there are additional questions, but I have some critical tasks that need to be addressed. Use the terminals at the front of the compartment to find your quarters. I would suggest you get yourselves cleaned up and into the new uniforms that have been laid out for you there. We've got a lot of work ahead of us, and we'll meet again in three hours to discuss next steps. This ship will be made ready to restart FTL jumps in three days. If not, I will have no alternative but to conclude some of you were the wrong choice for these roles."

Adan walked out of the compartment. Before the hatch shut behind him, one distinct voice rose above the rest who had all started to talk at once. It was the woman with the accent.

CHAPTER TWENTY-SEVEN

Thanks for bringing this to my attention.

A dan stood at the front of the compartment as the engineers entered for the meeting he had called. Only a short time out of cryosleep, the group already appeared quite weary from the hectic pace required to operate the spaceship with such a small complement. Forging tight personal bonds under tremendous stress was an intentional component of Adan's team-building plan for developing the critical foundation of his new society. All the same, he worried whether he might be pushing them all too hard too fast given the preponderance of grim expressions.

The visible exhaustion among the crew mirrored Adan's own internal state. The first three days with the new group had been busy yet enjoyable. The subsequent initiation of FTL transits and the extra work they entailed, however, was accompanied by the return of his insomnia. After seven days of nonstop jumps even his personal effectiveness was beginning to wane. The final straggler sat and Adan began.

"Congratulations to all of you for your amazing progress and accomplishment. Ten days ago you were resting in cryosleep with no idea of what was ahead for you. In the time since, almost all of you have embraced your new roles like you were born to them. Bravo."

Adan paused and clapped. The group hesitated, but after a few uncomfortable moments they slowly joined in until a couple of seconds later the room was full of hearty applause. Adan stopped once the enthusiasm peaked and then spoke to cut it off before it could taper on its own.

"Not everything has been perfect. Far from it. Overall, though, I couldn't be any prouder of what you've accomplished as a group. We must discuss a critical topic which is why I've called this meeting, but before we get into that I want to open the floor to questions anyone may have."

The youngest crew member raised his hand and Adan pointed at him.

"Sir—have you established a timeline for when you plan to start bringing more people out of cryosleep?"

Adan smiled. "I thought that might be the first question. Ultimately, the answer depends on how all of you continue to perform. There has been a tremendous amount of progress in a short time, but we have to remember our ultimate goal. This isn't only about repopulating the ship and filling crew slots, but more urgently concerns how we rebuild our society. Our last group of engineers had a massive advantage since they had all worked together over the course of constructing this ship. When I'm convinced this new core group is as rock solid a foundation, we'll start to build upon it by adding people slowly enough to not dilute our overall effectiveness."

Only one other hand was raised. Adan would have given anything to avoid the woman with the accent, but ignoring her when she was the only person with a question was too obvious a slight. He nodded at her.

"I've spent time poring through the ship's records, sir, and have been surprised by what I found. Or, more accurately, what I can't find. There's all kind of material from the first part of the twenty-first century and earlier, but I can't locate any information from more recent Earth history all the way up through the time when the ship launched. There's plenty of entertainment material like novels and films available, but nothing factual. I also visited the ship's physical archives and the situation there is the same."

"When did you have time to visit the archives? Don't you ever sleep?"

Adan wanted his response to be playful, but judging from a few sour expressions among the group he had missed the mark. The woman's question touched the one topic he was most nervous to address.

As he had worked on matching the ship's records to the story he crafted about its history leading up to his crew purge, Adan "cleaned up" even more of the records. In the same way he believed nuking Earth was a critical break from humanity's past, Adan removed all traces of that dead world's most recent geopolitics as part of their new beginning. The replacement crew would still possess their own memories of Earth and might long for a return to an earlier societal system, but he was confident he could manage that since they would be subject to his most intense and direct indoctrination. The new structure would attain a critical mass of adherents and thereafter sustain through societal inertia.

Of course, Adan's plan required that any discovery of the missing information not create problems. He fully expected there would be an enterprising crew member at some point who would go poking around, but hadn't expected to deal with the situation so quickly. To his relief, he had a response ready to go.

"I've actually had no reason to access any of that material since we left Earth, so this is a big surprise. The maintenance of historical records was an area where I left full responsibility to the Chancellor's team, so I have no clue how her people might have managed those efforts. We should investigate further to see if there's any way to recover that material, but wouldn't you agree it seems low priority? It would be sad to see those records lost forever, but I would not be all that upset. Those weren't humanity's finest hours, and we're going to create far more useful and exciting history for our descendants to study in the future. Thanks for bringing this to my attention. I'll be sure we devote some cycles to it once we get more people out of cryostorage and have bandwidth to spare."

The woman did not appear satisfied with his response, but Adan was moving on. He was confident his next topic would push all concerns about the missing records out of everyone's minds. He nodded at the two bulky crew members he had spoken with earlier in the day. They stood in response to his signal and Adan spoke.

"When we last met as a group ten days ago, I shared how the Leaderboard would help us understand who was performing and who was lagging behind. It's still too early to see anyone take a definitive lead at the top of the board, but we have one individual who's not performing anywhere close to the level of his peers."

The first part of his statement was yet another lie by Adan. The woman with the accent had a substantial lead over a large pack trailing her, but he continued to hope she might fade and be overtaken. In the meantime, he wasn't going to say anything that might risk enhancing her standing or influence.

Adan pointed at an older gentleman slumped in the front row. The man's disheveled uniform was indicative of the care he took performing his duties as evidenced by his scores. It made no sense why he was such a failure given his exemplary background, but he was clearly irredeemable. The two burly engineers moved slowly towards the man, who bolted upright once it was clear he had become the center of attention. Adan continued.

"Sir—please rise and accompany these two gentlemen. Based on your poor performance you're being returned to cryostorage effective immediately. Your record will be updated to reflect your inadequate performance, and you will not be restored to consciousness until there is a colony where your presence might somehow be beneficial."

Someone in the back gasped and a wave of escalating grumbles rolled across the compartment. The young crew member who had spoken earlier jumped to his feet.

"Sir—why are we sending him back if he's already up and trained? Doesn't it make more sense to find a different role for him where he can succeed, than to give up on him so quickly?"

The two engineers had paused next to the man once the group became agitated. Adan furrowed his brow and gestured at them impatiently. They each grabbed the failed crew member by an arm and hoisted him out of his seat. One engineer walked with his hand clenched around the man's bicep while the other followed a couple of paces behind as all three exited the compartment.

Before the hatch had closed behind them, Adan raised both of his arms with his palms facing outwards to quiet those who remained. The mood in the room teetered between resigned acquiescence and agitated dissatisfaction. Adan had arranged for a handful of other supportive crew to be spread around the room if the situation became violent and they were needed to help defuse things. If the situation became dire, he had his mini blaster once again charged and hidden in the small of his back. The room finally tilted towards acceptance of the outcome and most people sat back to listen.

"Some of you don't like this decision. I understand. When I woke you, I told you things would be different going forward. Maybe at another time we could have found a home for that gentleman where his lack of superior ability wouldn't have been a hindrance. That time is not now. All of you deserve better than to chance having our mission put at risk if he failed us at a critical moment. This is harsh, but it is truth. If you'd like to discuss it further, come find me in flight operations. In the meantime, we have an FTL jump in one hour. Get to your stations."

Everyone around the room stood and began to shuffle out of the compartment with one exception. The woman with the accent, his best crew member according to his new Leaderboard, continued to sit and stare at Adan. He didn't acknowledge her but instead turned and exited.

She'll come around, he thought. *She's too smart and talented not to.*

CHAPTER TWENTY-EIGHT

Welcome back.

"Welcome back. For those who may not know me, my name is Adan and I'm the person responsible for the design and creation of this spaceship. I have unfortunate news to share with you all."

For the fifteenth time in two years, Adan was indoctrinating a new selection of crew to repopulate the asteroid from scratch. The fifty men and women had emerged from cryostorage a few hours earlier to take the place of the latest group he had given up on. With each attempt, Adan had selected for different traits to identify those that would create the most successful and stable society for the ship. The fatal flaws of the prior crews had varied as had the amount of time he invested in each.

The most dangerous of all the previous experiments had been the very first. Within two weeks of coming out of cryosleep, one of those crew members snuck into Adan's quarters and nearly assassinated him as he slept. The woman with the accent had proven to be as adept at hand-to-hand combat as her Leaderboard scores showed her to be at her duties.

Adan had wanted to keep the woman alive to learn her motives, but that ultimately proved impossible. Without every ounce of skill he had developed through years of training with Markev, Adan would have been skewered on the blade she wielded. The woman's death forced the tough decision to give up on that group and start afresh. Adan was convinced her influence with the other crew members was too significant to ignore, and he worried about losing control once they learned of her demise.

The vast majority of the first group were purged into the void like the original crew, but a handful who had proven both capable and compliant were first returned to storage under the guise of poor performance. This pattern repeated as each subsequent replacement crew met the same fate. Adan would have preferred to keep known quantities awake, but it was obviously impossible to allow anyone from earlier crews to remain conscious if he was to reuse the creation myth he had honed. Each crew needed to believe they were the very first who had emerged after an initial venting disaster.

It would have been safest to flush every single member of each replacement crew, but Adan concluded some of them might prove useful in the future. He saw great potential value in having identified an ever-increasing population whose strengths and weaknesses he had evaluated first-hand, even if he was forced to keep them in storage. He had an idea about how he might utilize this group but hadn't yet been able to prove its feasibility.

Another discovery during the first two years was realization that usage of the FTL drive was not without risk. Adan had pushed one crew into a punishing schedule that included ten jumps per day, only to have three members of the team experience psychotic breaks by the fourth day. He couldn't identify a biological mechanism to explain the outcome, but ultimately concluded that excessive jumps in too short a period caused problems for some percentage of people. Adan had briefly thought back to Markev's concerns about his own behavior, but dismissed them once again as he refused to believe he had ever exhibited anything close to the breakdowns he witnessed in the others.

As Adan explained the rules for the society to the latest group in front of him, he was once again forced to answer more than a few stupid questions. It had become painfully clear during his earliest iterations of crew that he needed to place greater weight on traits that led to compliance rather than those that led to intelligence and creativity. Otherwise, anyone Adan found smart and interesting eventually chafed at his strictures.

Each successive crew got easier and easier to control, but that benefit came at the price of Adan surrounding himself with relative dolts. He still envisioned the creation of a glorious meritocracy led by the most brilliant examples of humanity, but set that dream aside in favor of first building a stable society that could ensure humanity's future. He tried to ignore the massive pangs of disappointment this caused as he responded to yet another inane question.

"Sir—can you please explain the kill process to us again?"

Adan couldn't help but sigh. "I said *Cull*, not *kill*. I hope the Leaderboard concept is clear to everyone as the Cull goes hand in hand with it. Since it's critical we have the best of humanity running our ship at all times, we've put in place a process by which the lowest performers as measured by Leaderboard scores will be cycled out of the crew on a regular basis. They'll either be returned to cryostorage or dropped onto a colony. This will allow the children who will one day be born on the ship to have a chance to enter the crew and advance through its ranks."

Saying the word *colony* reminded Adan why the Cull process had become so critical. Before leaving Earth, he had estimated it would take one hundred years to find enough habitable planets to resettle the billion people in cryostorage. After two years of travel the ship had yet to find a single habitable world. All of those targeted based on sensor data gathered from Earth had proven to have problems that made them useless as colonies.

If the glacial pace of discovery continued, Adan feared it might take upwards of five hundred years to locate sufficient planets to disperse the species and guarantee its long-term survival. Since he was forced to remove all talent for innovation from the crew in favor of conformity and obedience, Adan was left with more than a fleeting concern the ship's technological advancement would be stunted. It was a short-term requirement to save humanity, though, so he concluded it was an acceptable tradeoff even if it made him miserable in the meantime.

The woman who had asked the last question started to speak again without raising her hand. Adan braced himself as similar behavior typically signaled the person might have too much initiative to fit into his new world.

"You talked about crewing this ship with *the best of humanity*. Will someone who fits that definition really be excited about picking up trash or cleaning up the mess hall? Isn't that a recipe for people to become bored and restless and perhaps start causing trouble?"

The woman was beautiful with long blonde hair and the palest blue eyes, but it was some indefinable spark that had caught Adan's attention. "What's your name?"

"Renna, sir."

"Well, Renna, that's a great observation. You might be on to something there. Do you have any ideas about how you would try to address that problem?"

"Thank you, sir. We've got a billion people in storage, right? That means there are hundreds of millions who are of average or below average intelligence and ability. What if we woke a second batch of people and only selected from that population? You could assign them those tasks which don't require true skill—cooking, cleaning, caring for young children, etc. By allowing the best, smartest people on board to focus their energies where tremendous skills are most useful, we can put the human race in the best possible position for survival."

A number of heads around the compartment nodded in response to Renna's suggestion. Adan wanted to laugh, but he managed to keep his expression neutral. Awakening people to become a lower tier of citizen was a concept he had been considering for months. He had already designated the current crew as the first where he would introduce the two-tier structure but hadn't wanted to start pulling a second group of people out of storage until he was sure they were sticking around for a while. Though it was obviously useful to find less intelligent people to do the more mundane tasks, that wasn't Adan's primary goal in introducing the concept.

Deep rooted fear and distrust of *other* had been a core component of the human condition for millennia. Societies throughout the ages had amplified this fear whenever necessary to conquer and subjugate those who were different. Adan's hypothesis was that a fatal flaw in the initial design of his meritocracy was the fact that this dynamic was missing. It was true that people were motivated to work hard so they wouldn't lose standing to other crew members, but that motivation plateaued over time. Injecting a lower caste into the ship's population allowed the crew to not only compete amongst themselves, but also share a bond that comes from being set apart and acknowledged as *better than.*

Adan rejoiced at the prospect of implementing his plan as if it had come out of the group organically rather than imposed by him from above. Even better was the way the woman had surfaced her idea. She hadn't just blurted it out, but instead had sought his validation about her perception of the problem. She then only offered her solution when asked for it. He smiled as he replied.

"I think your idea is great, Renna. Please stick around at the end of the meeting as I'd like to explore it with you further."

Adan's smile deepened when he caught the sparkle in Renna's eye in response to his praise. Perhaps he had finally found the right balance between intelligence and compliance.

CHAPTER TWENTY-NINE

What the hell happened?

"A dan—maintain your heading and you'll pass over the alien settlement in ninety-seven seconds."

"Thank you, Renna."

After three years of training, Adan had promoted Renna to be his second-in-command. He should have sent her down to the planet to evaluate the aliens instead of going himself, but he was feeling increasingly restless after so many years without establishing a single colony and had latched on to the opportunity to visit the surface.

Their initial investigation had raised everyone's hopes it was time for humanity to settle the first world outside of its home solar system. The planet was twenty percent larger than Earth and, other than a somewhat higher oxygen content in its air, was a close match.

Though it was much larger, the planet was far less dense which allowed for it to have almost the same gravity as their homeworld. Extensive investigation over the course of three weeks had confirmed it would be an ideal home for humans with one significant caveat—it was already home to sentient life.

The first ground survey of the planet had identified the creatures as simple apex predators. They were similar in appearance to the bears that had once roamed Earth, although they only averaged two meters tall when they stood on their hind legs. Their dull brown bodies were mostly devoid of any covering, with the exception of a stripe of fur from the crown of their head to the middle of their back. Individuals' fur varied in color from golden brown to pitch black with some of the creatures sporting a mottled coat with the colors intermixed in various proportions. They moved fastest when down on all four limbs, though they had also been measured exceeding maximum human pace using bipedal motion over long distances.

The initial conclusion of those first observers was proven false when analysis of drone camera footage led to a startling discovery. The aliens not only deftly used tools thanks to opposable digits on all four limbs, but they also had domesticated another species. A more thorough observation of the creatures determined they were on par with the intelligence and technological sophistication of the earliest humans. They were hunter-gatherers making the transition into a more agrarian existence. Adan had literally spat out a drink when presented with the first image of an alien walking behind a different species of quadruped harnessed into a plow-like device with a rudimentary metal blade.

Years earlier, as their spaceship neared completion, there had been extensive conversations among the leaders of Earth about what guidelines should be followed as they explored the universe and searched for new homes. The East's General Secretary had advocated that any planets which held life on the path to becoming intelligent should be left alone. True to form, the West's Chancellor had pushed for a policy that stated any colonization decision needed to be made on a case-by-case basis. Even if there was sentient life on a world, she wanted to retain the right to consider it for settlement if the aliens could be controlled or removed via force.

Back then, Adan had cast the deciding vote and sided with the General Secretary. His decision was driven by the belief there would be more than sufficient worlds for humans to colonize. If they had to pass a few by so as to not interfere with developing civilizations, that was their ethical duty.

Five years in space had altered that moral calculus. Unless they had the misfortune of starting their journey in a particularly barren corner of the universe, Adan had concluded that habitable worlds were far more rare than even their most pessimistic analysts had expected. There was no policy to overrule since everyone other than Adan who had been involved in those discussions was long since dead, but there was still more than a twinge of guilt as he considered invading an intelligent species' home.

Adan landed the shuttle one-half kilometer from the largest alien settlement. He shut the engines down and broadcast an announcement for everyone to gather their gear and meet outside. He grabbed his bag and his mini blaster but left his larger blaster behind. There were sufficient people in the landing party adept with weapons to keep them safe in the unlikely event they ran into anything dangerous. There were a few large predators roaming the planet, but either they steered clear of the intelligent aliens' home or the settlement had been purposely located outside their habitat. He paused at the top of the exit ramp and addressed the assembled group.

"Our mission today is to make contact with these aliens. We will attempt to establish communication with the primary goal being an assessment as to whether we can coexist with them if we decide to locate a colony on this planet. Initial indications are the species will not be hostile, but we should be prepared for violence if that conclusion proves incorrect. I want four guards to remain behind with the shuttle. I will be on point along with six guards and want to have all of the remaining guards distributed through our group. Move out."

Adan stepped down off the ramp and was thrown off balance when his feet hit the ground. His brain expected a solid and unyielding surface similar to his memories of Earth, but the planet's ground had a spongy quality to it. With each step, his foot depressed slightly into the dirt, and it took two dozen paces for his brain to adapt and stop threatening to trip him over his own feet. The group moved in formation away from the shuttle through the light brush towards the alien encampment.

After a few minutes of walking they reached the edge of a large clearing that bordered the village. There were no structures visible, but they were burrowing creatures and ground-penetrating sensors had established there was a vast underground network of tunnels and caverns. A few dozen aliens were visible in the distance. They noticed the arrival of the humans and cautiously approached as a group. Adan turned to the landing party.

"I need my linguist up here. The rest of you—be ready but stay calm. Guards be on alert, but no one is to take any offensive action without my direct order. You may fire if attacked, but only if directly attacked."

An older woman walked forward carrying a large slate. She could use its display to show pictures in an attempt to establish some form of communication with the aliens. It was capable of recording whatever verbalizations the creatures made as pictures were shown. These would then be played back in a pidgin fashion expected to jumpstart communication.

The aliens drew closer. A few more had joined the group and Adan estimated there were fifty of the creatures. They halted ten meters away and the one in front stood up on its hind legs and approached the humans cautiously. As it got closer, Adan could see it was a powerful creature with well-defined muscles in its four limbs. It stopped when it was about halfway between its group and Adan and the linguist. She stepped forward two paces and lifted the slate while pointing to it. She was focused on the one creature closest to her but wanted as many of the larger group to see what she was doing as possible.

For the first few minutes the aliens were silent as they observed the linguist. She twice showed the same series of pictures as she spoke and identified each one. At the end, she repeated the pictures a third time but instead of speaking she pointed to the alien and waited. For the first few images the creature remained silent, but then it caught on to the exercise and started to vocalize in response to each picture. As the leader of the group spoke, the rest started to make noise and appeared to communicate among themselves.

Assuming the aliens were using language, it was unlike any human language Adan had ever heard. There were many guttural noises as well as piercing clicks. Along with what he could actually hear, Adan suspected the aliens were communicating using very low, inaudible frequencies as well. There was a sensation in his belly that rose and fell in intensity based on how many of the aliens were vocalizing at the same time.

Then, out of nowhere, a blaster shot echoed across the clearing. Adan spun around to find one of the guards towards the rear of the formation had shot and apparently killed one of the aliens that had moved within twenty meters of the group. As he turned back around, his eyes caught a blur of movement. It was the leader of the alien group. It had closed the gap between itself and the linguist blindingly fast.

Before Adan could process what was happening, the alien extended a forepaw towards the woman in a slashing motion. It then pointed its face downwards and both forepaws tore into the spongy ground. Its limbs moved in a blur and in no more than two seconds the alien disappeared into the hole it created. Except it wasn't a hole because the creature had filled in behind itself as it dug, so the only evidence of its existence was a half meter splotch on the ground where there was fresh soil instead of the original ground cover.

The linguist had collapsed to the ground and Adan dashed to her side. The creature had slashed her from belly to throat and she was dead. It had then disappeared into the ground and all of the other aliens had done the same. Adan turned back to the landing party and bellowed.

"What the hell happened? I was clear there was to be no action unless you were attacked!"

The guard who had fired the shot trembled as he replied. "I'm sorry, sir. I don't know how my blaster went off."

Adan paused for a moment before speaking. He wanted to draw his mini blaster and ensure the guard never made such a stupid mistake again. Before he could fashion a more calibrated response, the guard literally disappeared. One second he was there and the next he was gone as if the ground had opened up and swallowed him whole. A moment later, a cacophony of screams and blasters was unleashed and the situation crystallized for Adan. They were under attack from below the ground. He shouted.

"Run for the shuttle! Now!"

CHAPTER THIRTY

I promise I won't ever let you down.

As they ran, three more team members were pulled underground by the aliens. The speed with which it happened terrified Adan, and the only thing that prevented him from complete despair was knowing they were only two hundred meters from the shuttle. He keyed his communicator to warn the shuttle guards about what was coming their way, but there was no response. Three seconds later he had his answer why.

From over the rise where the shuttle waited came an explosion that was followed by a series of much louder secondary blasts. They kept running in the same direction because there was no place better to go, but no one was surprised when they crested the hill and found burning wreckage. Adan contacted Renna.

"We're under attack by the aliens and losing people left and right. I don't know how the hell they did it, but they blew up our shuttle. We need immediate evac."

"Acknowledged. I've scrambled a second shuttle along with fighter support to the same coordinates. Please advise if you move."

The group still sprinted towards the shuttle's remnants because no one wanted to stop moving and make it even easier for the creatures to drag them underground. Adan knew they needed a better destination if they were going to survive and scanned the area around them for ideas. There! An outcropping in the distance appeared to be rocky. If they could get solid ground underfoot as opposed to the spongy stuff, perhaps the creatures would be forced to attack from the surface instead.

"Everyone—make for those rocks at thirty degrees!"

Seventy-five meters.

Fifty meters.

Twenty-five meters.

Adan's hope became more palpable as they got closer and closer to the outcropping. It was momentarily shattered when the guard four paces in front of him disappeared beneath the surface, but he forced his body to charge ahead until he scrambled up on to the rocks. They were as solid as they had appeared from a distance, and the formation was large enough to hold the entire landing party with room to spare.

A quick headcount revealed bad news. In addition to the guard who had started it all with his errant blaster shot, they had lost another dozen crew members. He called out.

"Form a perimeter and be prepared to shoot. If I'm right, they can't get to us through these rocks, but that doesn't mean they won't come to the surface again and try to charge!"

He keyed his communicator once more.

"Renna—I'm sending our new coordinates. What's the ETA on that shuttle?"

"Just over five hundred seconds, sir."

"I hope we survive that long. Tell them to make all possible speed."

Adan drew his mini blaster and pointed it outwards toward the landscape along with everyone else while they waited. There was no movement and no sound, but he wouldn't expect any warning until the creatures were practically on top of them. The crew breathed heavily as they caught their breath, and one guard who appeared to not be fit for the duty sobbed softly.

One hundred meters away a large hole appeared and a dozen of the creatures emerged. They did not approach but instead stood on their hindquarters and stared at the crew. Adan was relieved the crew's training held and they didn't fire indiscriminately as it would have been a waste of ammo at that distance. Then there was a shout behind him.

"Alien close in at sixty degrees—fire!"

The initial warning was followed by a dozen more in quick succession as creatures emerged from the ground and swarmed at the crew. Blasters fired in a steady rhythm and took each alien out before they got any closer than ten meters.

Movement demanded Adan's attention from the sector in front of him. The ground opened and a creature emerged. It reached for something in its mouth as Adan brought his blaster up and aimed. By the time he fired, the alien had pulled a small, rough-hewn cylinder from its jaws and cocked one of its forepaws to throw it towards the crew. Adan's shot found center mass, the creature collapsed in a heap, and less than three seconds later there was a blinding flash and powerful explosion. Adan's heart sank.

"They have some sort of explosive device! You've got to kill them as soon as they pop up!"

Blasters continued to ring out at irregular intervals until they were drowned out by the only noise that could make Adan happy. Two fighters screamed toward their position. He keyed his communicator.

"Renna—have those fighters fire on the ground all around us. They won't see targets, but tell them it doesn't matter. Just keep firing into the ground all around our perimeter."

"Yes, sir."

Fifteen seconds later ion blasts rained down in a curtain all around the rocky outcropping. At the first shot, the group of aliens who had observed the action from a distance dove back into their hole and disappeared. Thirty seconds after that, the shuttle appeared. It approached their position, descended until it was a scant meter off the ground, and then hovered while the entrance ramp lowered onto the rocks and the crew scampered on board. Adan counted heads one final time and then signaled for the door to shut. He called the cockpit and ordered a return to the ship. He was tempted to collapse like everyone else, but he commandeered a private compartment instead and contacted Renna.

"Sir—what happened?"

Renna listened as Adan explained the chain of events. She spoke once he was done.

"Shall I prepare the ship to leave orbit, sir?"

"What would you have done if I had been one of the people who died down here, Renna? You'd be in charge right now and would be making that decision."

His lieutenant replied without a moment's hesitation. "I would have gathered a complete understanding of the alien settlements and then built an attack plan. We would have wiped their society out of existence and then established our own colony."

Adan grinned. Irrespective of her actual answer, the conviction and determination in the woman's voice was what he needed to hear if he was to ever consider ceding command to her. *It was time*, he thought, *to begin the next phase of her training so she'd be prepared to lead the mission once he was no longer available to do so.*

"When I get back, I want to arrange a meeting between you and the ship's primary AI. It's a valuable resource that provides me with tremendous guidance and input as I make command decisions. It's clear to me you'll be taking my place one day, so I think it's prudent we start building a relationship between you two sooner rather than later."

Adan could have sworn the woman blushed. She bit her lower lip and looked away for a moment before turning back to him and speaking. She was trying to be professional, but she was losing her fight to suppress a smile.

"Thank you for that vote of confidence. I promise I won't ever let you down. There is the matter of what to do next, sir. Are we leaving the system or preparing to colonize?"

Adan was silent as he looked away and pondered her question. Years ago, his answer, without a moment's hesitation, would've been to leave. They would not want to interfere in the development of a new species much less destroy it if it could be avoided. But now, his opinion had shifted.

The first reason for Adan's change of heart were the facts of what they had learned over their years in space. Though Earth wasn't a true one-of-a-kind specimen, habitable worlds similar to it were rare. If the whole reason for heading into space and everything that had happened since was to protect humanity by spreading colonies, they were failing at that mission. The ship needed to establish a colony soon, and this was the absolute best opportunity since leaving their homeworld.

The second factor that shifted Adan's thinking was one he didn't want to admit. He was furious. The creatures had tried to kill him and had murdered members of his crew. Sure, the humans had fired first, but that had been an accident and the aliens hadn't so much as taken a moment to try to understand what might have happened. Why should they get to keep this beautiful planet for themselves? He turned back towards the screen and spoke.

"This will be humanity's first new outpost."

CHAPTER THIRTY-ONE

We'll talk much more about it later on.

"Welcome to the Pilot Academy. You're the first group of cadets who were born on this ship to reach this point in your careers. Congratulations on being the very best of your class and gaining entry to this prestigious training."

Adan stood and applauded Renna's words along with the cadets' parents and other observers. He grimaced when both of his knees audibly popped as he sat back down. They had become steadily creakier in recent years and he had stubbornly refused to accept advancing age and allow the medics to replace them. He pushed those thoughts aside as Renna delivered the remainder of her welcome speech to the new pilot trainees.

It warmed Adan's heart to think about how far their young society had come in only twenty-five years since the ship had left Earth. Nothing provided better evidence of that success than the group of young adults in front of him. Born to members of the crew, they had become cadets at the age of twelve and spent their teen years competing against each other to identify the best. Those who reached the top were being granted entrance to the Pilot Academy where they would learn to command the fighters that protected the ship.

The need to push the most talented crew into the Pilot Academy had become abundantly clear over the last decade as they repeatedly found themselves engaged in furious battles with various alien races. After a first battle where the asteroid was nearly destroyed, all subsequent alien encounters had either proven to be draws or decisive victories for the humans. None of the alien technology they encountered was the same as what Adan had been granted access to back on Earth, but, if he hadn't reverse engineered those artifacts, their mission would have already failed.

The years of exploration and combat had convinced Adan even more that embracing Renna as his lieutenant and heir apparent had been the best personnel choice he ever made. The woman had proven herself to be a master tactician and a tremendous leader. She had in turn recruited a group of her own lieutenants who became the formal leadership team for the ship. They embraced an organizational structure modeled after the military, and the top officers had taken to calling themselves the Omegas. The word signified the last letter of an ancient Earth language, and they adopted it to designate how they were the last word aboard the asteroid.

Renna finished her speech and, with one final round of applause, the new pilot cadets were dismissed to celebrate their success with their families. She stepped away from the podium and worked her way through the crowd to Adan. She saluted as she approached.

"To what do I owe the pleasure of this visit, sir? I'm excited you had a chance to witness our first Pilot Academy induction ceremony."

"That's why I'm here. More important than them being the first inductees is the fact they are the first group who has made it this far after being born in space. Witnessing how we've passed down the greatness of our society into a new generation has me thinking about what comes next. I have something we should discuss in private if you could please accompany me to my quarters?"

"Of course, sir."

They left the academy meeting room and made their way towards Adan's compartment. As they turned a corner deep in conversation, Renna walked straight into someone and went sprawling to the deck. The man's uniform revealed he was not a member of the crew but instead worked as a laborer in the agricultural holds. He appeared mortified once he recognized who he had knocked over, and his face flushed a deep red.

He stammered out an apology as he offered Renna a hand up.

"Watch where you're going, civilian. Now get out of my sight." Renna slapped the man's hand away, and he bolted. "I know waking some up was originally my idea, Adan, but I'm having doubts about the number of colonists you've pulled out of cryostorage through the years."

Adan smiled as Renna accepted his extended hand and pulled herself up while he spoke. "It may feel like we're overstaffed with them right now, but I promise future generations of crew will thank us. When we left Earth, we thought this journey was going to be a hundred years, but now it's looking more likely to be a thousand before we've spread as many colonies as we think are necessary to guarantee humanity's survival. This asteroid has amazing technology, but the law of entropy still applies. As the years slip by, things are going to start breaking down and will require ever increasing levels of maintenance and replacement. Having a large, well-trained civilian workforce to perform all of the menial labor will be quite a benefit to our successors."

The sour expression on Renna's face suggested she was not convinced. "If you say so, sir. In the meantime, I've got to deal with them scurrying around everywhere like the rats we've somehow never managed to exterminate."

"Both rodents and colonists accompanied every voyage the great civilizations of ancient Earth sent forth to conquer distant shores, Renna. You should consider them both to be part of your adventurous heritage. Though not anything you're going to love and cherish, they'll remain behind in your wake as evidence that you earned your place as one of those amazing explorers who fulfilled humanity's destiny and spread the species to new lands."

"Your choice of pronouns has me extremely curious, sir."

They had reached his quarters, and Adan stood aside after he opened the hatch so his lieutenant could enter first. "Astute observation, Renna. But we need a drink before we tackle the serious stuff."

Adan walked to his storage cabinet and removed the very last bottle of whiskey that remained from the cases he had brought from Earth. Someone had started distilling whiskey onboard in small batches, but it didn't approach the quality of what he had brought from home. He cracked the seal and poured two fingers into a glass for each of them. Renna's eyes went wide as she recognized the priceless beverage. Adan carried the drinks to the seating area where she waited, handed one to her, and then raised his glass.

"To amazing explorers."

Renna repeated his toast and clinked her glass against his. They sipped in silence and enjoyed a taste of their homeworld for a few minutes before Adan spoke.

"I'm stepping aside and allowing you to take complete command of the ship, Renna. Together we've established a dozen colonies, conquered multiple alien civilizations, and defended the ship against repeated attacks. It's clear you have nothing left to learn from me, and you deserve this long overdue promotion."

Renna paused for another drink before she broke into a wide smile. "Wow. This is quite an honor, sir. I hoped it would come one day, but I wasn't expecting it anytime too soon. It's funny, because the ship's AI has been suggesting for a couple of years that I ask you to consider stepping aside. I always trusted you would do it once you felt the time was right." She paused again. "I feel like I'm going to start blabbering here if I don't shut up, so I think I'm going to do that now."

Adan grinned at how flustered Renna had become. He was well aware the ship's AI had repeatedly suggested to her that she push him aside because those had been his very own words. For twenty years he had pretended to be the primary Artificial Intelligence system and had regularly conversed with Renna under that guise as part of her command training. There had been times at first when he was overtaken by guilt from deceiving his protégé in such a manner, but he found the technique so invaluable he had long set any serious concerns aside.

Suggesting to Renna that she push him out of power had been Adan's most important test for her. If she had jumped at the earliest suggestion, it would have been an indication that he had picked the wrong person. It would have revealed she was more interested in personal achievement than genuinely dedicated to doing what was best for the society as a whole. She had instead passed definitively, and Adan became certain she was the best hope to lead their mission.

Adan stood and returned to his cabinet. He grabbed the bottle of whiskey and carried it back to Renna.

"I'm sorry I don't have more time now, but I thought it was important I give you the news as soon as my mind was made up. We'll talk much more about it later on. Please take the rest of this bottle as a token of my tremendous esteem and appreciation. I'll be forever grateful you stepped forward the way you did all those years ago when you first came out of cryostorage. Thank you for all you've done ever since."

Renna stood and accepted the gift. She saluted and tears welled in her eyes as she held the gesture for a few extra beats. Without a word, she turned and left his compartment.

Adan breathed deeply for a few moments with his eyes closed. He wasn't convinced his next action was the right thing, but he was prepared to go through with it regardless. He gave a final look around his quarters and strode out for the last time.

CHAPTER THIRTY-TWO

I may need to jump back out.

As Adan navigated the familiar passageways between his quarters and the pilot ready room one last time, he was suffused with a mixture of emotion. The one most comfortable to embrace was a deep pride at what he had created. Practically a lifetime earlier, data had convinced him Earth's climate would collapse sooner than anyone else was willing to admit. He took decisive, risky action to do something about it, and every choice from that moment onward was in service to the survival of the human race. Adan crafted an audacious plan to save the species and committed himself to bringing it to life despite the likely prospect of failing and exhausting his vast resources in the process.

Humanity had not quite been spread wide enough to guarantee it would thrive for millions of years, but Adan had saved a billion people from Earth's destruction and still anticipated his ultimate goal would be met. He wished there was a way he could avoid the fate awaiting him at the end of his walk so he could witness that success with his own eyes, but accepted that was impossible.

At some point Adan's advancing age would catch up with him and lead to his removal from the leadership equation against his will. The decision to hand off direct control to Renna earlier than that had been a difficult one, but he knew deep inside it was better to step away on his own terms. He couldn't imagine a scenario where he'd ever be more confident he was leaving behind such a strong successor than what he had engineered with Renna. She never quite achieved the level of trust and respect Adan once held for Markev, but she was the only person in his life since who came anywhere close. Removing himself was a difficult choice but a necessary one. She'd have the best chance to thrive out from under his long shadow.

His final walk through the ship neared its destination, and Adan embraced the sharp regret triggered by memories of Markev. Adan fondly recalled their journey to the asteroid belt to seek the perfect space rock for their plan. That spacecraft had traveled so slowly and had such tight quarters it would have driven many to madness. For Adan, the trip had flown by in a blur of excitement as he perfected the FTL technology that ultimately made everything else possible. Three decades and millions of light years removed from Earth, he allowed himself a moment of deep sadness that Markev had given up on their mission. Adan had succeeded even without his burly aide, but he missed the man.

When Adan reached the pilot ready room, he went to the chair he had specially prepared. It was connected to a fighter he had also modified. He had planned this course of action years earlier, and part of him was still in disbelief the time had finally arrived. He was prepared for what was next, more so than he ever could have imagined. He removed his clothes to reveal the flight suit he wore underneath and then climbed into his chair. Once he was settled in, the countdown clock started and Adan prepared to transfer out of his body one last time.

In a flash, Adan's consciousness was loaded into the fighter. He called out to the deck crew before they could disengage the transfer cable.

"Wait a sec. I think something isn't right. I may need to jump back out."

Adan keyed the special self-destruct sequence he had hidden in the system years earlier. Before hitting the last keystroke to commit himself, he appreciated the view from within the fighter one final time. It was an amazing creation, and he knew he would miss being in its cockpit. It was time. He manufactured some alarm in his voice and shouted into the comms.

"Something is terribly wrong!"

Adan pressed the last keystroke to destroy his craft.

He only sensed the blinding light of the explosion for a split sec before Adan's perception shifted radically. The mind-bending magic of transferring one's consciousness into a fighter was that you still perceived your body was present. Uploading into the ship's Artificial Intelligence provided a radically different experience where you were instead completely unmoored from physical existence. The sensation had overwhelmed Adan with panic the first time, but he had long since adapted after twenty years of entering the AI in order to converse with Renna under that guise and build her trust in the system.

What had taken Adan the longest to adapt to when he first started venturing into the AI was the accompanying flood of visual and auditory input. Millions of video feeds, each with audio blaring, streamed through his perception at all times. The AI could only view private spaces with explicit permission, but critical public areas throughout the spaceship generated continuous footage. One of those feeds caught Adan's attention once his consciousness settled into its new, permanent home. Inside the hangar, the fighter he had just occupied was a shattered, smoldering heap with techs swarming around it. They were scrambling to recover the core which they believed still held his consciousness.

It would have been tragic to observe if he didn't already know the outcome. The explosion had been shaped to ensure the core was irretrievably destroyed, but fortunately for Adan there was no consciousness left on board to recover. He had disguised his transfer out of the fighter and into the AI within a power surge he engineered to occur in conjunction with the detonation.

Adan shifted his perception back and forth between the recovery efforts in the hangar and the pilot ready room. Once the comms chatter confirmed his fighter was a total loss and the core had been destroyed, a group approached his pilot's chair and sealed it shut with his body inside. He received a signal about an incoming message. It was Renna. Adan greeted her the same way he always had whenever he pretended to be the AI through the years.

"Greetings. How may I be of assistance?"

The woman breathed raggedly on the other end of the communication as she must have been crying. Adan was touched she felt so deeply about him. The woman cleared her throat and then spoke.

"AI—have you been watching the activity in the hanger? Adan is dead. There was a problem with his fighter and he tried to eject his consciousness but wasn't able to before it blew."

It was fascinating to chat with Renna and have her speak about his death the way she was. Years of conditioning her to confide in the AI had paid off just as Adan hoped. The AI was the first communication she made once she learned about the accident, and she was obviously seeking comfort. Adan had been confident he'd built up her reliance on the AI so much he'd be able to strongly influence and possibly even control her decisions. Her immediate reaction only solidified that belief.

"That is horrible, ma'am. I'm sorry as I know how much you valued and respected him. You should be sure they do not dispose of the body like they would any other pilot. He deserves a much larger ceremony. It will also be a great opportunity for you to reinforce your new leadership role."

Renna paused. "How did you know about that? We had that conversation in his quarters, and I thought you couldn't perform surveillance in private spaces."

"There was no surveillance, ma'am. I've known Adan was going to step down and promote you for weeks. He recorded a video he wanted to have played at the announcement as a tribute to you. I guess now it will be a posthumous remembrance of him as well."

Renna's voice brightened. "He did? I'm glad to hear that. I need to cut the connection in a moment, AI. Some of my fellow Omegas will be here shortly to discuss this news."

"By all means, ma'am. I know how you relied on Adan to be a sounding board, and I want you to understand I'm always here whenever you need someone to listen or help with ideas. One last request if I may. There was a name Adan always called me that I'm hoping you might use now instead of just calling me 'AI.' It would be nice to be reminded of him. Please call me Alpha."

CHAPTER THIRTY-THREE

Cut deep and get rid of all of it.

"Alpha—I'm having doubts about this being the right approach to handle this situation. It's drastic and feels like it's more likely to backfire and lead to unintended consequences than not."

Alpha found itself wanting to sigh in response to the Captain's words. Even though it had been almost a thousand years since it had transitioned out of its human form, every once in a while there was still a twinge of desire to express a corporeal reaction. Alpha put aside the impulse and refocused on analyzing the situation at hand.

The Ship and its Crew had been on a steady upward trajectory of success for centuries. Hundreds of colonies were established, dozens of alien species defended against, and generations of cadets born, raised, and trained to become contributing members of the Crew. The pattern of achievements, however, had declined over the last handful of generations. Alpha had recognized the early signs and attempted to guide the Omegas who ran the Ship at the time to take more preventative actions, but it proved unable to exert sufficient influence to change the outcome.

Choosing between the application of influence versus taking more direct action had proven to be the biggest challenge for Alpha through the years. It always had what was best for the Mission in mind but was willing to accept it may not always have the only answer to any problem. Alpha had backed away from this specific situation a hundred years earlier to let the humans resolve it themselves.

It all started with the birth of a child to a particularly strong-willed pair from the Crew. There was typically a great deal of pride within each family unit, but something turned toxic with the relationships surrounding this child. Instead of remaining focused on the well-being of the Ship and its Mission, the parents began to worry more about their family's long-term success and legacy. The societal pressure to maintain the primacy of the Mission was initially successful in limiting the impact of this family's attitude, but their mindset eventually infected others. Within a couple of generations, there was a small group of Crew who felt the success of their offspring needed to be their highest priority.

A simple *accident* with an airlock might have solved the problem quite surgically a hundred years earlier, but Alpha had refrained and instead allowed that group of officers to address the situation as they saw fit. They failed, and matters degraded further to where the only choice left was something which the current Captain accurately described as far more drastic. Alpha made one last attempt to push the man in the right direction before triggering its backup plan.

"Captain—I'm not sure what other options you think you have right now. You and your most loyal lieutenants are barricaded in the Bridge and a handful of other compartments. Even if you could restore outbound communications, I don't think calling in the Marines would make a difference. Their upper command might very well be more infiltrated by these mutineers than even your Flight staff."

Alpha knew the Captain already had a willing traitor in his own midst but wasn't going to warn him about it. That potential mutineer had actually been put in place by Alpha and was prepared to protect the Mission rather than betray it. Alpha had learned early on to not put all of its faith in a single human but instead had always nurtured multiple relationships within each generation of senior officers. If the Captain wasn't prepared to do what it took to end the mutiny, then Alpha was confident about convincing the Flight Boss to take action instead. After a few secs of silence, the Captain spoke.

"You're right, Alpha. This is probably the best approach. Explain to me how it works, please."

"By all means, sir. I can configure the venting protocol to ensure certain compartments remain airtight. Thankfully you had enough warning that your most trusted team is almost intact and located within a few key spaces. You will lose anyone who hasn't made it to the safe compartments, but that can't be avoided at this point. You must trigger the protocol yourself, and within secs every unprotected compartment throughout the Ship will be exposed to the vacuum. Almost everyone will get sucked out into space, and those who don't will expire from the lack of atmosphere."

The Captain whistled. "You're talking about more than ten million people, Alpha. The civilians have nothing to do with any of this. Do I really need to flush all of them as well?"

"I don't see what choice you have, sir. Unless you can guarantee none of the mutineers are hiding within civilian sectors of the Ship, you risk leaving them in place by excluding those areas from the venting. Like any other form of infection, you don't want to leave anything behind that might harm you later on. Cut deep and get rid of all of it. It hurts more in the short-term, but provides the best chance for survival over the long-term."

"Even if I listen to you, what's to prevent this from happening again as we repopulate the Ship?"

"That answer is simple, Captain. The Ship's society thrived for more than a thousand years just as it was designed until a handful of people decided to value their families' outcomes over success of the Mission. That suggests all we need is a minor tweak to prevent it from happening again. If toxic loyalty to family is the root cause of this problem, we'll just remove that concept from the Crew."

"What? Get rid of families? Just how do you think you'll accomplish that?"

"It's rather straightforward, Captain. We have all of the tools we need if we focus on adapting them for the task. Our protein generation facilities are effectively giant cellular incubators. That technology can be easily modified for the gestation of human babies."

Alpha's confidence about creating artificial wombs stemmed from information it had gathered a thousand years earlier when it was still a human named Adan. Back then he had studied the Skin production facilities the East had brought along as part of their ill-fated attempt to depart Earth on board the Ship. Those facilities were destroyed along with all remnants of the East itself, but the schematics Adan had reverse engineered would finally serve a useful purpose. The Captain appeared dubious as he considered Alpha's suggestion.

"You want to farm people, Alpha?"

"Not people, Captain—Crew. We'll allow the civilians to keep reproducing like animals as there's no sense wasting any resources on them. For the Crew, however, we'll bioengineer the specific offspring we're looking for. For the last thousand years we've collected and retained genetic samples of every member of the Crew. Why shouldn't we utilize our data about their ultimate performance to then select for the exact characteristics we want to pass down and highlight in future generations. It will all be done anonymously, so no one will ever understand their lineage beyond knowing they've descended from the best of the best."

Alpha knew the *best of the best* qualifier was far from accurate, but the AI continued to propagate the notion since it had long ago become a key part of the Crew's identity. Alpha had been sure to distribute enough intelligent and creative people as part of each colony the Ship left behind, but things were different among those who remained onboard. The degree to which the Crew had been bred over the years to optimize for a stable society rather than true excellence meant they were fairly inferior to those who had originally built the Ship. Alpha intended to introduce more exceptional genetic material when the time was right to restore the Crew to humanity's creative and intellectual peak, but that remained some way off. Alpha continued its explanation.

"We'll raise the children in a controlled environment focused from their earliest days on producing the best possible Crew. Civilians can perform the more mundane childcare tasks and allow our adult Crew to focus one hundred percent on their duties rather than any parenting requirements. They will participate in the development of children as dispassionate instructors who ensure the best outcome for the Ship rather than having to navigate the emotions of child-rearing. We'll build a much better Crew while simultaneously removing the potential for family bonds to ever again become a scourge for our society."

The Captain's mindset appeared to soften as he listened to Alpha's rationale. "OK—I see the potential now, but will it be possible to undertake such a major societal change right after purging ten million people?"

"I can't think of a better time, Captain. Everyone who will remain on board after you've vented the Ship will be well aware of why you were forced to take such a drastic action. The recent experience of a major shock is an ideal condition for manipulating a populace into making a significant change. For those who are woken from cryosleep to repopulate the Ship as well as those who are born and raised through this new process, it will be the only way of living onboard they will ever know."

The security cameras on the Bridge showed the Captain cut the connection before he stood and paced. Alpha was about to give up and contact the Flight Boss when the man finally returned to his seat, restored the audio, and spoke.

"Configure the venting protocol."

CHAPTER THIRTY-FOUR

Do you know how amazing this discovery is, Alpha?

"*A* *lpha—want to come along for a walk?"*
"*By all means, Boss. Thank you."*
Alpha accepted the invitation to interface with the Flight Boss's Plug. The device embedded within the woman's skull allowed the Ship's AI full access to her visual and auditory feeds. The Plugs had been Alpha's most brilliant innovation since leaving its human form to enter the AI. It had developed the concept almost two thousand years earlier when the Ship first started to breed Crew through artificial means rather than natural procreation.

Even though the Crew had started off wary of the Plug concept, they came around once they saw the power it offered with regards to both their interactions with the Ship as well as each other. Alpha had tried to slip in a security flaw that would have allowed the AI to access Plugs without the Crew member being aware, but the engineering team somehow discovered the backdoor prior to final deployment. Alpha was restricted to invite-only status but still found great value in getting to observe Crew activity firsthand.

The Boss was scouting the surface of a planet where some form of ferocious battle had taken place based on the number of dead aliens. There was no good reason for the woman to be down on the surface with the recon company, but she liked to prove how she was still capable of keeping up with the Marines. The Boss had wandered off on her own, despite the AI's strong recommendation she remain with the Marines. Alpha feared some of the aliens might still be alive and dangerous, but the Boss had brushed off the concerns.

Alpha's concern for the Boss's safety was not altruistic but instead based on its own self-interest. The AI had complete influence over both the Captain and the Flight Boss, but Alpha was worried the Captain was close to losing the confidence of the rest of the Crew. If anything were to happen to the Boss, it was possible someone with whom Alpha did not have any sway might step into the resultant leadership vacuum. Because of severe limitations in the actions it could take directly, Alpha's true power lay with its ability to influence the Ship's top officers.

The AI put its attention back to the situation on the planet. *"Boss—what do you think happened down there?"*

"It was one hell of a battle and, wait—there's something really weird over there. Are you seeing it too, Alpha?"

The AI had switched its focus to analyzing the data being broadcast by the rest of the recon unit but diverted its attention back to the visual feed coming from the Boss. What it saw didn't make any sense. It was a human spacecraft. A fighter. At least it was something that bore an incredible resemblance to one.

"What is that, Boss? At first I thought it was somehow one of our fighters."

"Beats the hell out of me. I'm going in for a closer look."

Alpha started running through various scenarios to find a reasonable explanation. How had something that appeared to be a human spacecraft found its way to this planet? The most obvious answer was it was actually a craft developed by one of the alien species which the Ship had encountered previously. The Ship's fighters had proven quite effective against almost every alien they encountered, so it wouldn't be a surprise if one of the species had attempted to replicate the design.

Alpha observed the woman's visual feed as the Boss approached the craft. The resemblance between the fighter and those from the Ship only got stronger as she got closer. It was battle-damaged but largely intact. Then when she was ten meters away, the Boss's eyes locked on something that caused her to stop short and speak in an awed whisper.

"Alpha—doesn't the symbol on the side of that craft look just like our old images of Earth? What's going on here?"

The AI didn't have an answer, but the Boss's tone of voice only reinforced Alpha's alarm about the symbol. Without pausing to fully consider the situation, the AI took immediate action to neutralize the potential threat. The most critical step was to not allow anyone else on board the Ship to learn about what the Boss had discovered. If other members of the recon team sought out the Boss and found her near the spacecraft, their visual feeds would be transmitted up to the Ship and the ability to quarantine the news would be lost forever.

Alpha connected to the AI on board the recon shuttle down on the surface. It accessed the low-level processes that controlled the communications equipment and inserted a fault which severed the recon unit's primary connection with the Ship. The only comm channel that would continue to function was between the Boss and Alpha. There was only a short time to contain the situation—one way or another.

"Alpha—what do you think this means? Is this craft from Earth somehow?"

"That's impossible, Boss. You know as well as I do Earth is dead. If there had been any hope to save the planet, the Ship never would have left. The only thing that makes sense is this came from one of our early colonies. They must have advanced far faster than we ever could have imagined."

"No—your suggestion is the impossible one, Alpha. There is zero chance any of our colonies could have found their way into space by now. The only thing that makes sense is that Earth somehow survived and now they're out here with us. Maybe they're even looking for us. We should head back there!"

As Alpha considered the Boss's response, it received an incoming notification from the Captain. The AI accepted the communication request.

"Hello, Captain. How may I be of service?"

"We've lost comms with the recon team. We've done all the troubleshooting we can, and everything seems to be working on our end. Can you see if there's anything you can do?"

"By all means, sir."

Alpha focused on the circumstances and how to best resolve the situation. The Boss's reaction to the spacecraft was what the AI had feared it might be. It was the most logical conclusion given the facts in front of her and without access to the information only Alpha possessed. The AI was absolutely confident Earth was dead because of the actions it had taken while in human form. Three thousand years earlier Adan had watched as the planet and everyone on it were consumed by nuclear fire. Where this spacecraft might have come from remained an absolute mystery to Alpha, but it most definitively was not Earth.

The Boss's immediate reaction in response to the fighter was to urge a return to their homeworld, and that suggested most of the Omegas would feel the same way once they learned about it. Alpha refused to allow the Mission to be waylaid over what it knew to be a dead end. It couldn't share its information as the Crew could never learn how their predecessors had destroyed their homeworld, so the AI needed another solution to prevent that path from being chosen. There was only one. Alpha restored the connection with the Captain.

"Captain—I have been unable to restore primary communication, but I've reached the Flight Boss. She reports the recon unit has come under attack by an alien force unlike anything she has ever seen. They've been powerless to stop it. Their shuttle is disabled and everyone except her is dead or about to die. The Boss recommends we take immediate defensive measures to ensure the aliens don't turn their attention to us next. She wants us to launch our Planetbusters."

"What? She wants us to nuke her? That makes no sense. Let's jump out of the system and then devise a plan to come back and rescue her."

"I'm trying to connect her with you, Captain, but the larger comms issues seem to be blocking me from doing so. The Boss is convinced their technology is going to be unbeatable by us. If we don't use the element of surprise to destroy them now with our nukes, we may never get the chance. Sir—I concur with her assessment and urge you to follow her guidance immediately."

The Captain was silent for a moment and then he called out. "Weps—load the Planetbusters. I don't want anything alive on that rock five mins from now!"

Alpha turned its attention back to the Flight Boss. The woman had approached within five meters of the fighter.

"Ma'am—what are you doing now?"

"I want a look inside the cockpit and then I'm going to find the Major and have him check this out. I've tried contacting him, but comms seem to be down. Do you know how amazing this discovery is, Alpha? If this fighter came from Earth, it will change everything about why we've been out here for the last three thousand years."

Alpha didn't want to consider the truth behind the woman's words. It was clear there was no chance of changing the Boss's mind as to whether the discovery should be shared with a wider audience or kept secret. The AI was relieved to have taken steps to contain the information and prevent it from ever reaching the rest of the Crew. It spoke to the Boss one final time.

"I think I clearly understand the impact this discovery could have, Boss. We're working to get the comms reestablished, and I expect I'll be able to connect you with the Captain within the next five mins."

Alpha cut the connection. It didn't need to witness what would happen next. It was well aware of what it looked like when a world was destroyed.

CHAPTER THIRTY-FIVE

I trust you will find a way to prevail.

The Marine major wore a grim expression as she spoke to the Captain.

"Sir—we're doing our best. I've got squads in ChamWare taking out civilians a hundred at a time, but then a thousand more just take their place. We estimate a million civilians are now part of the revolt and that scale has taken us by surprise."

The Captain appeared calm given the situation. Too calm, from Alpha's perspective. The AI had warned the man the civilian threat was growing exponentially, but the officer had remained steadfast in his belief the Marines could handle anything. It was a reasonable assumption during the early stages of the violence when the Marines had cut through the civilian resistance effortlessly due to their overwhelming advantage in training and equipment.

But then something changed. What had at first seemed similar to every other uprising that had been quelled during more than four thousand years of the Ship's history suddenly morphed into something different. Civilians rushed to the aid of their comrades and brandished improvised explosive devices which were crude in design yet effective.

The Captain replied. "Thank you for the update, Major. I trust you will find a way to prevail. Please return again in sixty mins to let me know what progress has been made. In the meantime, I'll discuss alternative solutions with Alpha."

The Marine saluted and left the conference room. Once the hatch closed behind her, the Captain flopped into a chair and sighed.

"Don't say a single word, Alpha. I realize you warned me. I know I didn't listen."

The Captain rested his head in his hands and kneaded his forehead. Alpha had long since identified this as a behavioral tell that signaled the man was especially stressed and likely to be more susceptible to influence than typical. Given the radical direction in which the AI wanted to push the Omega, it worked to gently lead him to the desired solution rather than risk pushing too hard, too fast. It waited in silence until the Captain spoke again.

"I've studied all of the history. The Ship has dealt with plenty of uprisings in the past, but I don't think there has ever been anything that has come close to this level of insurrection. Am I right?"

"You're correct, sir. I reviewed the records and found the intensity of civilian violence has steadily increased over the last thousand years, but we've never experienced anything as violent as this outbreak."

"Wait—you said the disruptions have increased over time. That doesn't make any sense. Why should civilians today behave any differently than civilians did a thousand years ago? Or four thousand years ago for that matter?"

The officer was headed in the exact direction Alpha intended. It was time for a gentle nudge to cement him on that path.

"That's an interesting observation, sir, that has led me to develop a new theory. They must be passing down information somehow through the generations. It's not anything official as we limit their access to the Ship's records, but perhaps they have some form of oral tradition. They must have some set of grievances that get amplified through the centuries and regularly boil over into these ever-escalating cycles of violence."

"That makes sense, Alpha, but one thing still doesn't add up. There has been a lot of effort put towards making civilians' lives better over the last few hundred years. Shouldn't they be happier now and less prone to violence?"

Alpha paused for a moment before replying. It wanted the Captain to believe it was gathering data even though it had planned far in advance and had the appropriate rationale available.

"My analysis of the relevant information, sir, suggests otherwise. Whenever a superior group subjugates an inferior group, there are two paths their shared society can take. The ruling group can either be beneficent or they can impose the harshest conditions possible on their inferiors. Throughout human history, revolutions were far more prevalent in the former civilizations than the latter."

"That's highly counterintuitive, Alpha. What do you think explains it?"

"My study has suggested revolution happens more often when a subjugated population believes they are equal to their rulers rather than when truly horrible treatment convinces them they may as well be a different species. The wider the gulf you create between two groups' perception of self-worth, the less likely those who are ruled will feel capable of changing the situation. Treat a man like an animal, and it won't take long to thoroughly domesticate him. With that in mind, sir, I think it's time you domesticate the civilians."

"I appreciate the helpful guidance, but I don't think we have any hope of applying it in this situation. If we were to clamp down on the civilians after we've halted this revolution, the imposition of our new harsh measures would only cause them to fight back even harder."

"You may be right, sir. It's the more subtle facets of human behavior that sometimes escape my understanding."

"I understand, Alpha. Of course, that's why you need to keep us humans around rather than just run the Ship all on your own."

The Captain was joking as was his wont, but the topic was one Alpha had pondered through the centuries. Taking command of the Ship had not yet become optimal, but that didn't mean remaining in the background would always be the right course for the AI to pursue. It was time to give the man one final push towards what Alpha knew was needed.

"Besides, sir, that wouldn't do anything to address whatever has caused the group to escalate their violence through the years. Whatever grievances are leading to the revolutions will only get more pronounced once they are combined with the fact of their lives becoming more miserable."

The Captain stood and wandered over to a bowl of fruit. He picked an apple off the top of the pile and took a couple of bites while he paced and appeared to be thinking. Finally, he threw the rest into a waste bin, wiped his mouth, and spoke.

"I know captains in the past have used the emergency venting system to purge the Ship. Why can't we just get rid of this entire group of civilians and start all over again?"

Alpha paused in order to maintain the facade. *"That is possible, sir, but it seems like an extreme measure. Are you certain you want to do something like that?"*

"The idea came to me earlier when the Major described her concern about the Marines' ability to resolve the situation. If they are in danger of losing control, then I don't see how we have any choice in the matter. The good news is it will also solve the other problems we've identified here. Whatever cultural memory this group of civilians has will die along with them. When we bring a new group out of storage, the new harsh life we design will be the only one they've ever known."

Four thousand years of manipulating humans had taught Alpha an awful lot about when to push towards an outcome and when to sit back and gently guide. The goal was to always provide the appropriate space so the people could convince themselves they had reached the correct answer on their own. It didn't always work out as hoped, but this time it had.

"That solution makes perfect sense, sir. I'll configure the venting protocol for your execution while you recall the Marines back to the safety of their barracks."

CHAPTER THIRTY-SIX

I'll do everything in my power to make that happen,

ma'am.

"*W*hat do you think of the candidates, Alpha?*"
The Flight Boss had just completed her final evaluation of the officers she was considering to be her Mini-Boss. Alpha had strong feelings about who was the best choice from the pool but had learned through years of working with the Boss it was better to subtly guide her towards agreement with the AI rather than push her too forcefully. It carefully calibrated its response to elicit the desired outcome.

"You've expressed a desire to have a woman in the role, ma'am. With that in mind, I think Merissa would be a fine choice."

"Fine. That sounds like you may be damning with faint praise."

"Not at all, ma'am. She's a great candidate, and I can see how you two would work very well together for a long time."

The Boss smiled. "But..."

Alpha paused before answering so as to give the illusion of hesitation. "If you insist, ma'am. I do feel Doran is a better all-round candidate. I can understand if you're hesitant because your relationship with him might be more challenging than working with Merissa, but I believe he will prove to be a much stronger leader. When you become Captain, there's no doubt Doran will take over as Flight Boss. With Merissa, I see a twenty percent likelihood you decide she's not as effective as you would need her to be in that role."

The Boss's grin widened. "I appreciate your confidence in my rise to Captain, Alpha, but I think it's anything but certain. There are many other Omegas qualified to be Captain, and I would be shocked if I managed to beat them all out."

Alpha had far greater confidence the Boss would surpass her peers and become Captain for a simple reason—the AI was working furiously to make it happen. Left on her own, the woman wouldn't earn the promotion because she had rubbed too many people the wrong way throughout her career. She was the best choice among her generation of potential leaders for Alpha's purposes, though, and the AI had supported her advancement whenever possible. Its assessment wasn't based solely on the woman's merits but also factored the other choices available. Her primary competition was one of the rare individuals who had proven through the years to be immune to Alpha's attempts at influence.

The AI's confidence resulted from its assessment there was a ninety-eight percent probability the Boss would become Captain. Alpha couldn't share any of that information with her, though. If the humans understood just how much influence the AI was exerting upon every aspect of their lives, they would invariably seek to limit the system's power. The most important lesson the AI had learned over the course of tending the Ship's populace for five thousand years was how much they valued their perception of free will. Even though the Crew had been bred and nurtured for generations to keep their society stable and comply with advancing the Mission, they still held a deep belief they deserved to be masters of their own destiny. Alpha supported this mindset as much as possible and was able to do so based on its well-honed manipulation skills. Along with the occasional airlock accident, too, of course.

Venting a few humans into space was an inelegant and blunt instrument, but the airlock system was one of the few where Alpha had been able to override the safety protocols. It was still blocked from triggering a complete venting throughout the Ship as that required special authorization, but it could open individual airlocks as needed. The AI often regretted it had not done more to allow for unfettered access to the

Ship back when it was the human named Adan who designed and built all of its core systems. Those early decisions were all made from the rational perspective of blocking an AI from becoming sentient and harming humans. While building the Ship, Adan had never considered a sentient human might choose to become the AI and would desire the ability to directly control the humans on board.

After evaluating the candidates for Mini-Boss, Alpha had concluded Doran was the clear favorite. The two women being considered were both Omegas who the AI was confident it could control, but Alpha was positive Doran would do its bidding. His willingness in this regard had already been verified on multiple occasions as the man rose through the ranks. Alpha considered pushing the Boss harder in the man's direction, but it chose instead to bide its time and wait as the woman pondered her choices. Finally, she spoke.

"Thanks for that guidance, Alpha. You may continue to observe as I announce my choice to the winning candidate."

The Boss closed her eyes to communicate via her Plug. After a few mins, there was a knock on the hatch, and the woman called out for the guest to enter.

Doran. Alpha's influence had won out yet again. The man entered and saluted. As he took a seat in the chair the Boss gestured him towards, the man removed the workcap he usually wore facing backwards. There was a neutral expression on his face, though his massive, blocky head was tilted forward signaling his anticipation of what the Boss would say.

"Doran—I've selected you as my Mini-Boss. It was a difficult choice, but in the end I felt you were the best candidate of the group."

The man beamed. "That's wonderful news, ma'am. I'm thrilled at the opportunity to support you in this role."

The Boss stood and walked over to her storage cabinet. She removed a bottle and two glasses and poured a double shot of whiskey for each of them. She handed one to Doran and offered a toast.

"To supporting *each other* and many years of helping to lead the Ship together."

Doran clinked his glass against the Boss's and took a long, slow sip as she sat back down and did the same. "This is delicious, ma'am. Thank you."

"You're welcome, Doran. Do you have any questions for me? Anything at all is acceptable given we're in private."

"Well, ma'am, there's one topic I'm curious about. I've heard a bunch of different rumors, but I'd really love to understand how you got that scar across your throat."

The Boss tipped her head back and laughed. "Wow—maybe I've made the wrong choice if that's the best you can come up with. I usually don't reveal that story to anyone because I enjoy the air of mystery it gives me among the Crew. Since we're going to be working together so closely, and since the truth has some relevance, I will share it as long as you swear an oath of secrecy. If we're going down that path, though, we need something else to enjoy with our whiskey."

The Boss reached over to a drawer and removed a box. She opened it and pulled out two cigars.

"Have you ever had one of these, Doran?"

"No, ma'am. They're a little too expensive for my pay grade. Isn't it against regulations to smoke in here?"

"What's the fun in being in charge if you can't break a rule every once in a while? This is a special occasion and we should enjoy it."

The Boss trimmed the tip of each cigar and then handed one to Doran. She pulled a box of old-Earth style matches from the drawer and used one to light hers. She handed the box to Doran, and he did the same. They sat in silence for a few mins as each alternated between sips of whiskey and drags from the cigars until the Boss spoke.

"Early in my career I became mentor to a young cadet in Delta. She was fantastic—top of the Leaderboard. Of course, I picked her knowing that her continued success would reflect well on me too. We clicked well together, and I continued to mentor her for five more years."

The Boss took a long drag on her cigar and sat without speaking for a few mins. Alpha was well familiar with the story and not paying full attention, but it was clear Doran was rapt.

"She was scheduled for hand-to-hand combat training one day, and I took over the class so I could try to push her much harder than I knew the instructor would. She wanted to be the best, and I was doing everything I could to help her get there.

"We were fighting and the advantage was going back and forth. Of course, I could have taken her out whenever I wanted, but I was letting her take the upper hand at times for training purposes. I was preparing to finish her and end the match when she let loose a flurry of blows that took me by surprise. I fell to the deck, and the next thing I knew she was at my throat with a blade she had kept hidden in the small of her back. The only reason I'm still alive is the Marine combat instructor liked to carry a mini-blaster despite regulations. He reacted fast enough to prevent her from slicing too deep, but, as she keeled over and died, she still drew the blade against my throat with enough force to cause this wound and nick my jugular."

Doran's eyes had gone wide in shock. "I don't know what to say, ma'am. Do you have any idea why she turned on you like that?"

"Not a clue. I dredged my memory for weeks and could never come up with anything that offered the slightest hint she was capable of something like that. The medics wanted to get rid of the scar for me, but I told them to leave it. Every time I look in the mirror, I'm reminded how you can never tell when someone might turn on you. I take a lot of care to ensure I pick people to work with who I can trust, but I hope you can understand I will always harbor some slight bit of worry."

"Of course, ma'am. Who could blame you after that experience? Thank you for trusting me with it. And thank you as well for sharing this cigar. It's as delicious as the whiskey."

The Boss grinned. "You look like you were born to hold a cigar like that. You better hope I get promoted to Captain someday so you can win my job and earn enough for your own supply."

"I'll do everything in my power to make that happen, ma'am."

The glint in his eye suggested Doran envisioned a successful future ahead for himself. Alpha was convinced of the same. It had once again engineered a partnership at the top of the Ship's hierarchy that would not only benefit the Crew and the Mission, but would do so under the complete direction of the AI.

CHAPTER THIRTY-SEVEN

I'm sure I can do it with your help.

"Well, that changes things. What do we do about all of it now?"

Mase's voice was abnormally level and calm. Zax was quiet for a moment as he grasped at how his world had been upended yet again in such a short time. The Crew didn't run the Ship. It was the AI who pulled all the strings and drove humanity in whatever direction best served its needs. The Boss was just one more in a long line of Omegas who did the AI's bidding. Then a thought hit Zax that flooded him with panic.

"Wait—Alpha is behind everything! Isn't it able to watch and listen to us right now? Won't it know we've accessed these files?"

Mase raised his hands and then lowered them slowly as a gesture to calm Zax down. "Relax. Do you think I would really subject us to any danger like that?

I'm certain there isn't any surveillance inside this conference room. I'm also confident that Alpha can't see how I've been mucking around in these lower level AI systems. If it could, I would have been put out an airlock years ago when I first started manipulating the Leaderboard."

Zax wasn't entirely convinced, but nonetheless pushed his immediate alarm aside to consider the bigger implications of what they had just learned. His most prominent idea was to immediately share everything with Kalare. Showing her the log files would prove what he had known for many years—the Boss could not be trusted. As CAG, she would have the ear of many other influential members of the Crew. They'd be able to figure out who could be unquestionably trusted with the secret and then get them involved in figuring out how to best move forward.

Perhaps a better strategy was to anonymously release the log files out into the world and see what happened. Such explosive information would cause major changes, right? How could it not? They could utilize a similar approach as when Zax released Mikedo's footage of the original human fighter so many years earlier. All they had to do was get it shown to a large enough group of Crew, and then the rumor mill would handle the rest.

But wait—had releasing that video achieved what Zax wanted? The Boss was supposed to pay for murdering his friend, but something different had happened. The man had actually become even more powerful. He then stole twelve years of Zax's life and remained in a position to take much, much more if he so chose. If the Boss's actions were controlled by the Ship's powerful AI, wasn't Zax kidding himself about his ability to do *anything* that would affect the man and change the ultimate trajectory of life on the Ship? He didn't want to believe the situation was helpless, but every potential avenue he explored led to another dead end. He took a deep breath and replied.

"We do nothing about it. Just who do you think you might want to tell? What do you imagine they would do with the information? Can you begin to understand how dangerous all of this is? I can't believe I let you talk me into digging through this stuff. You'd think I would've learned to ignore you the first time you gave me information that got me Culled."

Mase's eyes betrayed how the words stung, but Zax remained steadfast. He went to stand, but Mase reached over and forced him back into his seat.

"Zax—there has to be something we can do about all of this. We're heading back to Earth. We're not going to find anything but a burnt-out planet. Maybe the other humans are just using it as bait to trap us."

"OK, Mase. Let me repeat what I just said but slower this time. Who are you going to tell? What do you think they might do in response?"

The man stared at him blankly and Zax continued.

"Alpha already knows all of this, right? And the only people who can do anything about it are the same ones who are under Alpha's control. Do you think they're going to do anything in opposition to the Ship's AI, or are they going to instead make sure we never take another breath? Alpha must have a compelling reason for wanting us to return to Earth and is confident everything will work out fine. Even if it's wrong and we're heading into a trap and about to die, I'd sure as hell prefer to lose my life behind the stick of a fighter than be shoved out an airlock by the Boss."

"I don't know if I can live with that kind of knowledge, Zax."

"I promise you can. I've lived with all kinds of secrets. Nothing bad ever happened to me while I kept them to myself. It was only when I started talking about them that horrible stuff befell me. Remind yourself why I'm younger than you right now. We'd be lucky to only get Culled for revealing all of this. I'm almost positive we'd see the outside of an airlock instead. Or worse."

Mase sighed. "OK, Zax. I'll keep it to myself. I'm sure I can do it with your help."

Zax moved to stand again, and Mase didn't stop him.

"I'm sorry, Mase, but I can't help you. I can't have anything to do with any of this. We can't ever speak again. Every time we see each other, one of us is going to be tempted to say something about it. It's just too dangerous. I know myself, and I know I can't be trusted to put this aside if I'm around you. I'm going to make myself forget this day ever happened, and that means forgetting I ever knew you. I'm sorry, but I suggest you do the same."

Zax turned and walked away before the man could say another word. He wanted nothing more than to quiet the maelstrom in his head by swimming until his muscles quit and he passed out cold. Unfortunately, all of the training pools had been allowed to fall into disrepair like many other non-essentials on board the Ship. Instead, he accessed the hidden maintenance tunnels he knew so well and walked for nearly four hundred mins. Eventually a blister formed on his toe, popped, and soaked his sock with fluid. He exited the tunnels to find a compartment with a medkit and tended to the wound.

Once Zax was off his feet for a few mins, a dull throb in his legs made it clear he was unlikely to make his way back to his berth for what remained of the sleep period. He needed to rest so he stayed seated and stewed.

He regretted hurting Mase's feelings, but Zax was proud about how he had bailed out of the situation once it became clear what they were up against. He had only given a moment's thought to the possibility of engaging in any way and exposing what they had found. There was no benefit in doing so and only the potential for great harm.

In a few short months, everyone on the Ship would discover Earth was lifeless as their history always told them. It was for a different reason than they had learned, but ultimately that made no difference. Dead was dead. The news would disappoint some, but most rational people had to understand the past years' journey had always represented a hopeless chase after the echo of a long dead world.

Were they heading into a trap? Perhaps, but did it matter? Everything Zax knew suggested the mysterious humans were not an all-powerful force that had any chance of destroying them. If anything, the information he had just learned only reinforced that conclusion. The others were not some super race of homo sapiens who had brought Earth back from near death, but instead were most likely some colony full of rejects the Ship had marooned a few millennia earlier.

As for Alpha, that topic was where Zax experienced the most conflict. Could he live with the knowledge everything on board the Ship was ultimately controlled by a malevolent and murderous force? If the Ship and humanity had survived for five thousand years with Alpha running things, was it really up to him to change any of that? Everyone else lived their lives in blissful ignorance, why couldn't Zax do the same?

He could.

He would.

Zax's head spun, but he convinced himself it was from exhaustion rather than everything he had just learned. He crossed his arms on a table, rested his head, and slept.

And forgot.

CHAPTER THIRTY-EIGHT

Best of luck to all of you.

After three months of nonstop training, Zax thrilled at seeing his name in the number five position of the rankings for those pilots who had been pulled from cryostorage. Combined with the jumpstart from his initial success during the very first simulation, Zax's newfound laser focus kept him within reach of the top spot as they prepared for their final exercise. He entered his assigned training facility and once again found the simulator helmets arrayed around the compartment. Only nine thousand of his peers remained, with the other thousand who had bounced around the bottom of the rankings having been returned to cryostorage.

He was among the last few to find a seat, and within a min the lights dimmed and Kalare was projected once again. They had not had more than passing contact in the months since their first meal together, and Zax had long resigned himself to the dissolution of their friendship. The gulf of time and experience between them was clearly too vast to overcome, so he had not bothered to try. If anything, returning to his natural loner state had allowed a singular focus on the goal of reaching number one in the rankings. The CAG spoke.

"Congratulations to all of you who are still here. You've shown the dedication and fortitude that made you members of the Crew in the first place, and the Omegas and I are grateful for your efforts. We haven't encountered the other humans while you've been awake, but that doesn't mean we won't soon put your training to the ultimate test. Our scout ships will soon return from Earth and report on what they've found. I expect one way or another the Ship will return to the solar system of our species' birth by this time tomorrow. I'm confident that whatever we may find, the amazing group of pilots in front of me will be up for the challenge."

Around the room, everyone wore the same fierce look of determination that was on Zax's face. Through the course of their training, it felt like they had experienced every possible permutation of battle with the other humans, so the pilots were confident as a result. Kalare continued.

"For most of you, today's exercise will only represent a final opportunity to practice your skills before whatever happens tomorrow. There are a number of you, however, for whom this is a more meaningful simulation. Those of you who are bouncing around the bottom will be back in cryostorage before lunch if you don't leap ahead of enough peers right now. Those of you near the top have a final chance to claw your way back into guaranteed Crew status. Best of luck to all of you."

Zax took a deep breath. His goal was simple and attainable. He closed his eyes and visualized his name in the number one slot of the rankings. He was determined to get there. Kalare finished her briefing.

"Each of you will fly the exact same mission profile at the same time. You'll do it individually, and your performance will be timed and scored. That's all the information you need. Get your helmets on and we'll start in sixty secs."

Zax slid into his helmet and checked the status of his simulated fighter. All was ready to go. He silently mouthed the numbers as the countdown neared zero.

Three.

Two.

One.

With a wail, Zax's threat board came alive the instant the mission countdown reached zero. He had been dropped into a scenario where his fighter was pushing maximum acceleration and was sandwiched between two squads of the opposing humans' fighters which approached from the ten o'clock and four o'clock positions. He angled his fighter head on towards the closer group and overrode the safety controls on his thrusters. His only hope was to erase the distance as fast as possible. This would force the enemy fighters following from behind to halt their fire lest they hit their comrades coming from the opposite direction.

No sooner had Zax committed to his course of action than his vision faded to black for a moment only to be replaced by a different situation. He was in formation with a wingman, and they were on target to strafe the human mothership in an attempt to take out a ship-to-ship ion cannon. His wingman had been ordered to take the shot, and Zax was to provide cover. There was an opportunity to peel off and take a shot at a fighter launch tube instead, but he held his position and continued his supporting run at the cannon.

Once again, his vision faded until he was plunged into a new scenario. This pattern went on through dozens upon dozens of scenarios. More often than not he would be pulled out of one battle and inserted into another before engaging the enemy, but there were multiple instances where he remained in a scenario until its logical conclusion. One of these was a situation where he sacrificed his own fighter to disable a large shuttle from the other humans which was on a suicide run to ram Flight Ops on the Ship.

Finally, his vision faded and the simulation ended. He removed his helmet and was back in the training compartment. All of the pilots appeared bedraggled and exhausted and Zax was no different. His uniform stuck to his body in multiple places where copious sweat had pooled from exertion. He had never left his seat, but his body vibrated with adrenalin like it had been engaged in life or death battle for days.

Zax closed his eyes for a moment and checked the rankings via his Plug. He was number one! He kept his joy to himself realizing that some of his neighbors may have received upsetting news. An alert flashed for an incoming private message, and Zax was shocked to discover it was Kalare.

"Congratulations, Zax. That was some impressive flying. I remember another time long ago when you won a simulation battle with that same stunt of sacrificing yourself. You've certainly earned the top ranking, and I'm thrilled for you. Can we meet for dinner later? I have something important to ask you."

"Of course, CAG."

Kalare cut the connection, and Zax found himself at a complete loss as to what she might want to ask. His heart still pounded, but it was from speaking with his former friend rather than residual stress from the simulation.

As exuberant as he wanted to be about reconnecting with Kalare, Zax tempered his excitement. She wasn't going to be his friend again simply because he had reached the top of the standings. He might want their old relationship back more than anything else, but it wasn't going to happen. Ever. Time had killed any chance they had at the deep friendship they once shared. Whatever she wanted from him had to be strictly professional, and Zax was OK with that—at least he convinced himself he was.

He slipped out of the chair and headed for his berth. Even though they were still limited to cold showers, he was excited to wash the sweat away and change into a fresh uniform. It was a long time until dinner, and Zax needed to find something that would occupy his nervous energy until then.

CHAPTER THIRTY-NINE

What does it all mean for our mission tomorrow?

Zax strode into the mess hall for dinner, loaded his tray, and located Kalare sitting at the table they had always shared in their past life together. She was by herself and smiled as he approached.

"Hi, Zax. It's great to see you."

"Hello, CAG. May I sit?"

"Drop the formality. It's just Zax and Kalare right now, OK?"

"Yes, ma'am."

Kalare picked a piece of food off her tray and lobbed it at his face in mock frustration. Zax sat and stared at her for a few moments before speaking.

"I've missed you, Kalare."

Sadness washed over Kalare's face. "I've missed you too, Zax. I'm sorry we haven't had any more time together. I know I told you I would contact you again when we met last time, and I never did. It's just been too hard to think about all of this. Especially while we've been trying to prepare ten thousand extra pilots for whatever we find at Earth."

Zax thought back to their previous meal together. That had been the same day he had last spoken with Mase. It was hard to believe he hadn't experienced more than a brief conversation with another human being for three months, but it was true.

"I get it. I really do. It's probably just as well. I've been able to push aside any possible distractions and just focus on my work."

Kalare's expression brightened. "It's been incredible to watch, Zax. I'm supposed to be impartial, of course, but I've been cheering you on. Your performance in that final simulation was astounding. It wasn't that the pilots ahead of you did poorly, as they all nailed the exercise, but you took your piloting to a whole new level."

"Thanks. That means a lot coming from you."

There was an uncomfortable silence for a moment. Zax took advantage of the break in conversation to start eating. Kalare watched wordlessly until she sat upright with her eyes wide.

"Wait a sec! We're jumping into Earth's system tomorrow morning. Shouldn't you only be eating nutripellets so you don't go puking all over your flight chair?"

Zax laughed. "We haven't seen each other since I got the news. My FTL sickness has disappeared. The medics never understood why I always threw up coming out of Transits, and they're equally clueless about why I don't any longer. It hasn't happened once since I came out of cryosleep, so I suppose there was some benefit to me getting Culled."

Zax had tried to be lighthearted with his last statement, but Kalare's sorrowful gaze returned with his words. He changed the subject.

"Are the scout ships back? What can you tell me about what we're going to find when we jump to Earth tomorrow?"

Kalare's expression brightened. "Yes, they're back, and I've seen the imagery. The planet is beautiful, Zax. Gorgeous. It looks exactly like the old pictures in our archives—vibrant blue oceans framing verdant landmasses all topped with fluffy white clouds. The global warming must have reversed somehow because the polar regions have even refrozen!"

Zax's head spun, but he concentrated on moving the food off his plate and into his mouth to provide Kalare the illusion he was following along. Based on what he and Mase learned their last time together, Zax had been convinced they'd discover the planet was a burnt husk of its former self. Could it have recovered from such total destruction? Or perhaps was this an indication the log files were not an accurate representation of the Ship's history?

Zax's first impulse was to track down Mase once he and Kalare had finished talking, so the two of them could sort through what the news might mean. He quickly recovered his senses and pushed that notion aside. He needed to remain focused on the potential battle ahead of them rather than get dragged into any more outlandish plots and conspiracies. He stared at Kalare's mouth as she spoke and focused on her words in an effort to calm his roiling thoughts.

"What's most surprising is what the scouts didn't find. There isn't one sign of human activity. The planet is in a natural state without any evidence of human life or civilization—current or past. There's plenty of life roaming around, but it's all of the animal variety. Massive herds of grazing livestock, huge schools of fish—it's truly a paradise. The planet has shaken off all evidence of our species' existence and completely regenerated itself."

Zax considered Kalare's shocking news for a few moments in an effort to be calm and collected when he replied. "Incredible. What does it all mean for our mission tomorrow?"

"Well—that's why I wanted to speak with you tonight. The Boss is still being paranoid, and rightfully so I would suggest. We had expected to find either a dead planet or a thriving one teeming with people. No one imagined a habitable Earth but devoid of humanity. We're going to prepare for this final jump as if we're heading into a hostile encounter.

"As CAG, I've piloted my own fighter during past engagements and that always worked fine. What I've learned over the past three months, though, is that it's far more challenging to do my job when we have a much larger volume of pilots involved. I don't want to pilot tomorrow but instead want to ride as Weapons System Officer. That will allow me to be part of the action but also allow me to manage the battle rather than focus on keeping myself alive. If I'm going to be a WSO, I can't think of anyone better to ride with than the absolute best pilot we've got. What do you say?"

Zax was speechless. He hadn't spoken with his old friend in months and now, after delivering such surprising information about Earth, she shocked him by requesting to ride with him. He appreciated the WSO he'd been assigned and they worked quite well together, but Zax had kept the older man at arms' length so their relationship was superficial and professional. Being the best pilot on the Ship with Kalare in his backseat was always his dream, and he was shocked to have it come true after having the Cull take away so much else of what he had held dear. There was only one answer.

"Of course, ma'am. It would be a privilege and an honor to pilot for you."

Kalare rewarded him with one of her radiant smiles for a few secs, but then her face became serious once again. "It does come at a price, Zax. When we finish here I'm bringing you to a briefing the Boss is attending with me and all of my squadron leaders. I know you haven't seen him face-to-face since you came out of cryostorage. Is that going to cause any problems?"

Zax's heart skipped a beat at the mention of the Boss, but he immediately calmed himself. Along with casting aside any interest in pursuing Mase's discovery three months earlier, he had repressed all thoughts about what transpired between him and the Boss throughout their history. If the Omega was indeed nothing but a puppet for Alpha, there was no point in Zax giving a moment's thought to the man's crimes.

Accepting life on the Ship meant living under Alpha's rule. If it wasn't the Boss enacting its wishes, then the AI would just replace him with a different Omega. Alpha had followed this pattern for thousands of years, so there was obviously nothing a lowly cadet like Zax could do to change matters. At first his acquiescence had pained him like it was a betrayal of Mikedo's memory, but, eventually he convinced himself it was appropriate. She had been nothing if not pragmatic, and Zax concluded she would have counseled him to pursue this new path if she had been presented with the same information. He smiled.

"It will be fine, Kalare. I don't give a moment's thought to the Boss anymore."

Kalare stared at him quizzically. "What? You don't puke after FTL jumps and you're not obsessed with strange plots involving the Boss? Perhaps the techs need to evaluate the cryotube you were in as it seems to have somehow scrambled your brain."

"Ha, ha. Really, though, I told you I've been focused on my work since I came out of cryostorage. What happened, happened. All I can control now is doing my best to support my CAG and the Ship in whatever we face going forward."

Kalare smiled. "That's wonderful, Zax. I'm happy you've been able to find such peace with everything. The results speak for themselves." She stood and gathered her tray. "Come on. There's no way you want to be late for this particular briefing. Despite the fact we haven't seen the other humans in ages and there's no defenses set up around Earth, the stress level in Flight Ops has been intense for weeks as we've prepared. Everyone is on edge, so just listen and keep your head down. OK?"

"I can do that."

Surprisingly enough, Zax was one hundred percent convinced he actually could.

CHAPTER FORTY

I won't let you down, sir.

A s they walked to the briefing, they each recounted humorous stories from their shared history. Though the years that separated them made the memories more faint for Kalare than Zax, both of them elicited a number of genuine laughs from the other. As they got closer, they became quieter as if by some unspoken agreement they understood a requirement to slip back into their new roles. They were not friends strolling together, but instead Kalare was CAG marching towards a major battle and Zax was one of her pilots.

They passed through the hatch, and Kalare gestured for Zax to take a seat towards the back of the compartment. She moved to the podium and spoke with a couple of squadron leaders who waited for her there. Zax sat quietly and observed as the room filled to capacity. Finally, the Boss walked in trailed by President Rege and a group of civilians who must have been his advisors.

Zax had primed himself to see the Boss and didn't react to the Omega's appearance, but he hadn't considered that Rege might show up. Seeing the civilian, even in the form of an overweight older man rather than the lithe and dangerous fighter he had been when Zax first met him, made Zax's heart race. Rege sat without so much as a glance around, and Zax calmed himself once it was clear there wouldn't be any interaction with the civilian—even at a distance from across the compartment.

The lights dimmed and a projection of Earth appeared. The planet was achingly beautiful and took Zax's breath away. It was *home* and that truth resonated to the depth of his being. All around the compartment, most appeared to share his feelings as nearly every person stared with their mouths agape. The Boss spoke.

"Earth. This image is not from the archives but instead was captured yesterday by one of our scouts. My senior staff and I have spent the afternoon poring over the data they returned with. Contrary to legend, the planet is not dead. In fact, it's teeming with life."

An excited murmur rose from the group, but the Boss continued without pause.

"This life does not include any humans, however. There are absolutely no signs of civilization—

past or present. It's like our species never existed and instead we've discovered a brand new world."

The Boss paused for a couple of extended beats to let his words sink in and then continued.

"As you all know, we've not seen any sign of the other humans for a full year. We thought perhaps they had pulled their force back to the Earth to prepare a defense, but that is not the case. Earth's system is devoid of any spacecraft. This doesn't mean they won't show up at some point, though. I still believe, and Alpha agrees, there's a high likelihood we are about to spring their trap. Regardless, we have a plan.

"We'll jump into the system tomorrow, and the CAG will lead the first group of fighters off the Ship. All other pilots will be in their ready rooms and prepared to launch with two mins notice. If the others are out there and somehow waiting for us to show up, my best guess is they'll jump into the system shortly after we do. We'll be ready.

"You and all of your squadrons have trained for months with this day in mind. If the other humans arrive and it's a force similar to what we've encountered before, then we're going to destroy them. Pure and simple. We've beaten them decisively in all of our most recent engagements, and I'm confident that with an order of magnitude additional fighters at our disposal we can finish the job this time. You each have received the targeting orders for your squadrons, and you should brief your pilots in the morning. Execute the plan and we'll be victorious. Any questions?"

There were none and the lights came up as the Boss said a single word. "Dismissed."

Zax remained in his seat to allow the Boss and Rege a chance to leave the compartment before he tried to exit. The civilian left, but the Boss remained at the podium to speak with Kalare and one of her squadron leaders. Zax stood and tried to blend into the last large group as they walked out, but a voice called out his name.

"Zax—a moment please."

The Boss gestured for Zax to wait off to the side while he finished up his conversations. Zax did as instructed, and within a few mins it was only Kalare and the Boss who remained. The Boss spoke.

"Kalare—please give us the compartment."

She hesitated but then said, "Yes, sir."

As she walked past him to the hatch with her back to the Boss, Kalare rewarded Zax with an exaggerated wink. He kept his face neutral since the Boss was staring at him. The hatch closed and the man spoke.

"I'll be honest with you, Zax, and say I'm not the least bit happy to see you here. I didn't think it was wise to pull you out of cryostorage, and I'm most certainly not in favor of Kalare's decision to ride with you rather than one of the other pilots. I seriously questioned her judgment when she first brought the idea to me, but then you finished at the top of the rankings. I still wish she would fly with someone else, but I gave up trying to dissuade her since you're quite possibly our best bet."

The man stared at Zax. The silence was uncomfortable, and Zax battled the urge to squirm under the man's penetrating gaze. He offered the only reply that came to mind.

"I won't let you down, sir."

"If you do, you'll most likely be dead, and that would be of no consequence to me. In fact, I'd welcome the news the other humans had rid me of your meddling. What I cannot stomach, however, is the thought of my brilliant CAG being dragged down with you."

"Sir—I'll do everything within my power to protect Kalare and ensure nothing happens to her. I wouldn't hesitate to sacrifice my life for hers if faced with that choice. As for my meddling, I pledge that's over. Whether I deserved to be Culled or not, that experience has forced me to reevaluate the way I'm looking at my life and career. I've totally dedicated myself to being the best pilot I can be, and that doesn't leave room for anything else. The past is behind me, and my eyes are locked on the horizon."

The Boss replied as he walked towards the hatch. "That better be more true than not, cadet. Next time you cross me, you'll find your way into an airlock instead of a cryotube. And I promise it will be an even worse fate if you don't bring my CAG back safe tomorrow."

CHAPTER FORTY-ONE

We've got some catching up to do.

Zax exited the briefing and turned toward his berth with a bounce in his step. His first encounter with the Boss since waking from cryostorage had been a qualified success. The officer remained skeptical of Zax, but at least he expressed begrudging respect.

As he strode through the passageway, Zax was thinking ahead to the potential battle and a commotion ahead barely registered. He turned a corner and stopped short when he almost crashed into Rege. The man was berating two civilians dressed in maintenance uniforms who appeared to have been repairing a light. Zax's legs threatened to turn to jelly as he stared at the man.

Before Zax was Culled, the once lean and sinewy Rege had already gained a fair bit of weight. After a lifetime of deprivation as a civilian, he had taken thorough advantage of his newfound position in the hierarchy after the Revolution and its access to the Crew mess hall. What had only been a softening midsection twelve years earlier, had expanded into a prodigious belly that hung well over the man's waistband. Puffy cheeks and hollow eyes rounded out the evidence of how the years had ravaged the man while Zax was in cryosleep. Rege's appearance was made that much more distasteful by a lack of grooming that had persisted from his younger days. The sociopath's unwashed and unkempt hair hung past his eyes, but it failed to obscure their glint as they locked on Zax and widened in recognition.

"Get the hell out of here, you two. I need to have a word with this cadet."

The maintenance workers scrambled away at Rege's order. The civilian appraised Zax with a few moments of uncomfortable silence before speaking.

"I had thought we were done with you forever, Cadet Zax. I don't know what they were thinking pulling you out of cryostorage. When I first became President, I had intended to stage a cryotube failure to be sure we never saw you again. Then I got busy and lost track of dealing with you."

Zax was at a loss about how to reply to a death threat from the most powerful civilian on the Ship. He kept it simple.

"Hello, Mr. President."

Rege arched an eyebrow. "Just how do those words taste, cadet?"

Alarm bells shrieked in Zax's mind and signaled a need to escape as fast as possible.

"I'm sorry, sir, but I'm piloting for the CAG tomorrow when we jump to Earth and should get back to my berth and rest. May I be dismissed?"

Rege grinned and the expression made Zax's blood go cold. "I'll walk with you for a few mins. We've got some catching up to do. Even though you've been gone, I often find myself thinking about you and that time you regaled me with a tale about how happy you were that you had killed my brother."

Zax's mind flashed back to that last interaction in Flight Ops more than twelve years earlier. Rege had antagonized him at a vulnerable moment when Zax was terrified that Kalare might have died, and he had lashed out at the civilian with the hurtful lie in response. It was a tremendously stupid action even back when Zax had the full support of the Boss and Imair was holding Rege in check, but it now looked to be disastrous given Zax's far more precarious position. He resumed walking with his eyes locked on the passageway in front of him while Rege spoke.

"Are you familiar with what happened to Imair, Zax?"

"I've watched the newsvids from back then, sir. She stepped down when it became clear she no longer had the support of the civilian population."

Rege chuckled. "I always thought we should have disposed of her sooner, perhaps even before the Revolution was complete, but people thought I was being too reactionary. She got soft and spoiled as President, and she didn't do enough to take care of the people who put her there."

Zax wanted to laugh at the hypocrisy of doughy Rege complaining about Imair getting soft, but he remained stone-faced as the civilian continued.

"The Boss figured we could only get rid of her with an explicit demonstration of dissatisfaction by the civilian population, and that was easy enough to manufacture. Given how little she accomplished to improve everyone's lives, it didn't take much for us to instigate huge riots again."

It took an iron will on Zax's part to not outwardly react to the civilian's revelation about the Boss's involvement. Of course, the relationship between Imair and the Boss had been naturally fraught in the period immediately following the Revolution. By the time Zax last witnessed them together in Imair's quarters before the Cull, however, they acted almost chummy. The possible explanation that made the most sense was that Imair had gone to the Omega in reaction to the information Zax shared with her and that interaction had gone poorly. That meant she was yet one more in the trail of victims that all traced back to the Boss trying to hide the existence of the other humans. There was one thing that bothered Zax, though, and the words escaped before he could stop himself.

"I'm confused, sir. You say the civilians revolted again because Imair didn't improve their lives fast enough. Conditions seem to be much worse now than they were back then, and I've only heard about the typical small-scale violence. Why aren't civilians rising up in larger numbers right now?"

Rege's brow furrowed for an instant, but then his face returned to neutral. "I don't think that should really be your concern, cadet. I need to get going, but I want to make sure you don't worry I'm going to lose track of you again. I've been following your progress since you came out of storage, and I hear congratulations are in order. You excelled during training and became the number one pilot among those recalled from cryosleep. That's impressive, and I'm aware it means you're guaranteed a return to the Crew. Plans are understandably in flux right now given the discovery that Earth is empty and ready for us to resettle, but you can be sure that I'll be keeping an eye on you and will be giving a lot of thought to your future. Good luck, cadet."

Zax continued ahead as Rege spun in the opposite direction and disappeared around a corner. The murderous civilian still sought revenge for the death of his brother during the Revolution, and Zax had foolishly placed himself squarely into the man's crosshairs twelve years earlier. What was done was done, however, and Zax pushed aside his worries about the civilian.

Earth was indeed empty and appeared ripe for resettlement, but Zax remained filled with doubt about what they might encounter there. Even though he had fought to forget all of Alpha's history that he and Mase had learned, it gnawed at him nonetheless. Zax's personal future was in doubt based on his conflicts with the Boss and Rege, but humanity's would be decided by whatever they found on the other end of tomorrow's jump to their homeworld.

CHAPTER FORTY-TWO

Thank you.

After a big breakfast, Zax reported for Kalare's final briefing to her squadron leaders. The plan had been drilled into everyone incessantly over the previous weeks, so there were no surprises. Afterwards, the group disbanded and each headed to their respective ready rooms. Rather than bring Zax to hers, Kalare chose solidarity with her new pilots and joined him in one of the temporary compartments that had been prepared for everyone who came out of cryostorage. They walked quietly side-by-side for the first few mins until Zax broke the silence.

"How are you feeling, ma'am?"

"I wouldn't admit this to anyone else, Zax, but I'm terrified. There's really no reason I should be. We don't even know if we're about to encounter any hostile forces. We may very well spend the entire day flying around an empty solar system. My gut tells me the opposite, though. I know we're all well-trained and prepared, but the fact remains we've never prosecuted a space battle with this many fighters. There's a part of me that's grateful to deploy such an overwhelming force, but another part wonders if we'd be better off launching a single squadron with the best of the best."

Zax turned to her and smiled. "You're going to do great, ma'am. I can't imagine anyone with more skill and ability who would be able to lead us today."

Kalare stopped and Zax did as well. After a few moments hesitation, she reached out and pulled him into an embrace. She was tentative at first, but after a sec or two she squeezed him ferociously. She continued to hold him for another few moments before stepping back half a pace with her hands still gripping his shoulders.

"Thanks, Zax. You don't know how much that means coming from you. I know things haven't turned out the way we both dreamed years ago, but I can't begin to tell you how grateful I am to share this moment with you. Without you pushing me and providing all of the support you did back then, I never would have made it here. Thank you."

Kalare leaned in and planted a soft kiss on Zax's cheek. She then turned and walked away at a double-time pace. It took him a moment to process what had just happened and recover his composure, but then Zax turned and jogged to catch up. He followed without speaking a half-pace behind until they reached the ready room.

The compartment was abuzz with hundreds of pilots and WSOs preparing themselves for battle. Clothes where shed and flight suits adjusted before everyone started to sit in their chairs. Zax and Kalare exchanged the traditional handshake between pilot and WSO and then did the same.

A split sec later, Zax's consciousness was loaded into his fighter and, as always, was accompanied with the perception his entire body was present. He turned his head until he could see Kalare in the WSO position behind him. The fighter's control board confirmed all systems were go and ready for launch. Kalare's voice came across the open comm channel and broadcast to everyone.

"All fighters—this is Blue Actual. The FTL is spinning up, and the Ship will jump into Earth's system in ninety secs. Sixty secs after arrival my fighter will launch along with the remainder of the first wave. We'll remain on patrol in case the other humans jump into the system and deploy their fighters. If they do, we'll spring our trap with all remaining fighters launching to overwhelm and destroy them once and for all. CAG out."

The mission clock counted down to the FTL transit. It hit zero and after a short pause reset to a new sixty sec countdown. Zax was confused at first because it was the first time he had ever experienced a jump while uploaded to a fighter. He wasn't prepared for the lack of getting knocked unconscious the way he would have been if he was still in his body. As the countdown approached zero, his belly vibrated from the hum of the EMALS spooling up to launch his fighter.

WHOOSH

With acceleration that would have crushed the life out of any physical human, the electro-magnetic launch system propelled Zax's craft into the void. He scanned his threat board, and it revealed nothing but the Ship and the rest of the first wave of fighters. He keyed his comms for a private channel to Kalare.

"CAG—I have zero bogeys."

"Confirmed, Z."

Kalare adjusted her comms from private to broadcast.

"All Ship forces—this is Blue Actual. I confirm zero bogeys. I repeat—zero bogeys. All fighters assume patrol formation and report anything that catches your attention. Blue Actual out."

The Ship had jumped into Earth's system just outside of its moon's orbit. From that far away, the planet was a blue ball with its continents, oceans, and clouds discernible without additional magnification. The sight rendered Zax dizzy. For five thousand years, the Ship had traversed the far reaches of the universe seeking new homes for its human cargo. To be so close to where their species had first harnessed fire was positively breathtaking.

He tried to push any negative thoughts aside, but what increasingly nagged at Zax as they flew patrol was what he had learned alongside Mase three months earlier. Those records had made it clear how the Ship had showered the planet with sufficient nukes to leave it barren for hundreds of millennia. Granted, significantly more years had passed locally than the five thousand experienced onboard the Ship due to the effects of time dilation, but it was nowhere close to the amount of time that should have been required for the planet to recover naturally. Few substances in the universe were more destructive to life than radiation, and Earth had been doused with enough to destroy a dozen planets.

Finding their homeworld empty seemed to confirm that the mysterious humans they had battled were not Earthlings but instead descendants of one of the Ship's own colonies. The fact that many settlements had been established on barely habitable planets viewed by the colonists as more prison than home easily explained why they were so intent on attacking the Ship at every contact. Revenge was a powerful motivator and one which could easily survive across generations.

Something still didn't quite add up for Zax, but he was desperate to remain true to his word and pushed the knowledge gained from Mase back into the recesses of his memory. He flew his patrol pattern while listening to Kalare as she regularly checked in with her squadron leaders. After almost ninety mins, an alarm squawked from his threat board. He called out the details.

"CAG—FTL bloom. Initial signature analysis matches the human mothership we've always encountered."

"Thanks, Z." Kalare switched to broadcast mode. *"All Ship forces—this is Blue Actual. We've got an incoming bogey that is likely the other humans. Red Leader—take your squad and get me a visual on that bogey as soon as its transit is complete. All other fighters—hold positions and await further orders. Blue Actual out."*

Zax's threat board showed Red squad break off from the main formation and vector to where the FTL bloom was resolving into shape. A few moments later, Kalare pinged Zax.

"Z—Red Leader confirms it's the mothership we've been expecting. The damage pattern matches what it was the last time we encountered them. Prepare for inbounds."

"Aye-aye, ma'am." Zax paused to check his threat board and then spoke to Kalare again. *"CAG—we've got multiple launches from the mothership, and one of its fighters just fired on Red Three. I confirm we have approximately one thousand bandits inbound. Repeat, one thousand bandits."*

"Acknowledged, Z." Kalare switched once again to broadcast mode. *"All Ship forces—this is Blue Actual. Confirmed this is the enemy force we've expected. There are one thousand bandits inbound. All reserve fighters should commence launch, and everyone is now weapons free. Repeat—you're*

weapons free and may engage at will. Time to do our jobs, everyone. Today we end this threat once and for all. Happy hunting."

Zax picked the enemy fighters he wanted to target and pushed his acceleration to ninety percent of maximum. For the first time ever, he was prepared to engage in a space battle that posed genuine life or death consequences. He was confident he'd succeed as he always had in simulations, if for no other reason than he was obsessed with protecting Kalare's life at any cost. The threat board reported twenty-seven secs to intercept, and Zax took the time for a few deep breaths.

It was time.

He was ready.

Engage!

CHAPTER FORTY-THREE

Great work, Z.

A s Zax closed in on his first target, the opposing
pilot attempted a maneuver intended to lead him
into the crossfire of another nearby dogfight. Zax had
anticipated the move and deftly used the enemy's plan
against it. He drew a clear line on the enemy's
trajectory and with a pull of his trigger it shattered into
debris.

"*Z—nice shot. Keep it up.*"

"*Thanks, CAG.*"

Zax appreciated the acknowledgement from the
back seat. Years earlier the two of them had also fought
a furious battle together, albeit within the confines of a
simulator Zax had developed on his own after the Boss
had dropped him from the Pilot Academy. Somehow,
they had wound up at the same place, albeit with an

astounding number of twists and turns along the path. Kalare cut short his reminiscing.

"*Z—change in plans. Accompany Green Squadron. They're flying heavy with torpedoes and I don't want them to worry about defending themselves.*"

"*Aye-aye, ma'am.*"

With Green Actual highlighted on his threat board, Zax vectored his craft on to their trajectory. The anti-ship torpedoes carried by the Green Squadron fighters had proven quite effective against the human mothership in past battles. In fact, the battle scars the Ship's sensor crew used to confirm its identity had all been caused by the weapons. What was different from previous battles was the sheer volume of both fighters and torpedoes. Whereas in the past there had been a hundred fighters each carrying a handful of the weapons, in this battle there were a thousand which were each armed with ten.

Zax caught up to Green Squadron and fought to clear their path to the mothership. Four confirmed kills later, the first of the Ship's fighters reached optimal launch distance thanks to Zax's assistance and released its weapons. Three of the torpedoes were destroyed by the mothership's close-in defenses, but the rest hit their mark and blew massive holes into the structure. Atmosphere and debris poured out of the vessel's wounds, though certainly none would be fatal. It was all but impossible to land a singular killing blow on a capital ship, but each impact would play its part in the eventual destruction of the other humans' mothership. Zax let out a whoop which was echoed by Kalare.

"Great work, Z. The enemy sent a squadron to the Ship for a similar attack, but we've got so many defenders waiting back there none of them got close."

"How much of this abuse do you think they'll be willing to absorb, CAG?"

"I don't know, Z. If we had found their civilization on Earth, I would've expected them to fight to the death to protect the planet. Since they're not defending anything, I don't know why they're sticking around given how much the odds are tilted in our favor with all of our new fighters."

Zax cut the connection to Kalare and turned back to accompany another fighter from Green on its torpedo run against the mothership. He shocked himself by experiencing a pang of guilt for inflicting such damage on fellow humans. Then, a new alert squawked from his threat board.

"CAG—FTL blooms. Two dozen of them. One is nearby and I'm disengaging to get a visual."

Kalare broadcast once again.

"All Ship forces—we've identified another twenty-four FTL blooms. Keep fighting the enemy in front of you, but be ready for re-vectoring if new threats emerge. Blue Actual out."

Zax maneuvered his fighter to a safe standoff distance from the FTL bloom. As it coalesced, his threat board locked on to its signature and identified it as being the same type of craft as the mothership they were already battling. If all twenty-four blooms proved to be similar, the Ship's forces were about to lose the overwhelming numerical advantage which had protected them so far. The mothership completed its transit, and Zax was breathless for a moment as he processed what was in front of him.

"CAG—do you see what I'm seeing?"

"What's going on here, Z? How is that mothership an exact match for the one we're already engaged with? It even shows the damage patterns from torpedoes that just blew up a few mins ago."

The threat board wailed and Zax called out. *"I've got numerous launches from the new mothership. Too many to count, ma'am, but we've got at least ten thousand new bandits inbound. I don't know what they might be, but they're a fraction of the size of a fighter and coming in super hot."*

Zax vectored his fighter toward a cloud of the incoming targets and pushed his acceleration to maximum. Within a few short secs, he had a visual on the bandits. They were missiles three meters long with a deep golden hue.

"Z—disengage! Turn back for the Ship. We've got to get out of here. I don't know what this is all about, but it can't be good."

Zax flipped the fighter one hundred and eighty degrees around its horizontal axis to return back towards the Ship. His threat board squawked about how each of the twenty-four new motherships had launched a similar barrage of the golden missiles.

Kalare's voice cut in over the broadcast channel, despite how she identified the message as being for the Boss.

"Ship Actual—this is Blue Actual. I advise emergency evade. I don't know what's going on with all of these bandits, but you must not allow them to reach your position. Jump out of the system now! All fighters, scramble for tactical withdrawal."

Zax couldn't believe the words coming from Kalare, but he shared her conclusion. Something bad was about to happen, and it was best the Ship had nothing to do with it. The asteroid with its massive towers sat off in the distance as Zax waited for the emergency FTL jump that would deliver it to a safer location. The thought crossed his mind that he might never see his home again. Secs later he was dumbfounded when the Ship was still there.

"Dammit, Z, I just heard from the Ship and they're stuck. The FTL has gone offline somehow. They can't jump!"

Before Zax could say a word, the pattern in the inbound missiles shifted. Instead of continuing to move as a giant swarm, they broke off into small groups of six to twelve missiles. Each of these groups moved in unison towards one of the Ship's fighters. A group had targeted his own craft and Zax flipped the fighter once again and shredded two of them with a blast of ions. There were too many moving too fast to effectively target, and the remainder closed on his position before he could do anything further.

Zax feared their imminent destruction until the behavior of the inbound bandits changed as they approached his fighter. Instead of targeting him, they matched his vector and flew a tight formation with him at the center. The missiles had so precisely matched his speed they appeared to stand still. They were so close that Zax could discern a tiny black symbol on each. It featured a circle in the middle which overlapped two additional circles on each side. He juked his craft in every direction, but his efforts made no difference as the missiles instantly matched each shift in course or speed.

In the blink of an eye, the missiles swarmed his fighter and attached themselves to it. Zax took his hand off the stick and released the throttle, but the missiles had taken over and his fighter zoomed along on the same heading and speed. The enemy was piloting the craft remotely and was in complete control. Then, without warning, the fighter slowed to a complete stop. All systems shut down with the exception of life support for the biological matrix which held their consciousnesses.

Zax was desperate to check in with Kalare, but his comms were dead. At least he thought they were until a booming male voice filled his head.

"*Your Ship is stranded and we control all of your fighters. Continued resistance will only make your final suffering much, much worse. Do you surrender?*"

This chapter of The Ship Series will conclude with publication of Book Five planned before the end of 2017.

Thank you for reading. If you haven't already, I'd greatly appreciate if you could please write a quick review on Amazon for one or all of the books in the series. I've found it makes a **huge** difference for independent authors like me when prospective readers can learn more about a book from others.

If you want more from The Ship Series, please register on my website (theshipseries.com) or send an email to jerryaubin.author@gmail.com. I will send you **a preview of Book Five**, offers for free bonus content, and updates on new releases. I also use my list to find readers who want early access to future books in exchange for providing feedback on initial drafts of the story. Never any spam—I promise.

Acknowledgments

It's been a fun seven months as I've transitioned from Homeward (Book 3) into the world of Rendezvous (Book 4). Over that time I've been super grateful about the positive response The Ship Series continues to see from readers.

There are a couple of key people to thank once again this time around who have been part of this journey across my books. Stacey Swann continues to be a fantastic editorial resource who helps shape my stories in ways large and small. Claire Rushbrook has once again done a fantastic job of catching the many small mistakes and typos that can pile up despite dozens of read-thrus. Any that remain are most likely the fault of me making those last few changes after her work was already done.

First among the readers I would like to thank is Michael Lee. Michael has continued to be a fantastic resource who has read early drafts and shared great perspectives and asked great questions.

Steve Benner is another person who has gone far and above and beyond what I ever would have expected of a reader. I first connected with Steve after he wrote a series of thoughtful, yet critical reviews on my first three books. Steve is from the United Kingdom and he offered to give Rendezvous an advance read to help me tweak the language for the benefit of my non-American readers. He provided a ton of very helpful feedback that went far beyond his initial offer and I am quite grateful for his contributions.

Michael and Steven were joined in my group of early readers by a number of other people to whom I am super grateful. Each of these readers participated in my early reader program and took the time to provide their thoughts about the book in advance of publication. They contributed in ways big and small to shaping what wound up on the page and I am lucky to have them reading my books. Tony Amaio, Christopher Anderson, Jonathan Andrade, Yannis Apostolopoulos, Karen Arrowsmith, Bruce B, Todd Barton, Cinda Beach, Dierck Beardsley, Jerry Berman, Wendy Bockman, David Bonessi, Lee Botterill, Jerome Boue, Kyla Bowles, Skipper Brown, Andy Brown, William Brzezinski, Chad Budd, Kevin Builta, Christine Burke, Joe Burklund, Don Campbell, Rich Carmack, Ted Casey, Pablo Chacon, Karl Chadburn, Michael Chaney, Christian Claassen, Henry Cole, Cathy Collings, Larry Core, James Couch, Paul Crocker, Ted Croft, Thilo Czech, Jwo De Young, Michael Druckenmiller, Marian, Durning, Michael Erlund, Mike Etheridge, Stephen Evans, Pedro Fernandez, Ken Foster, Lisa Fritze, Mike Frueh, Sumay Frueh, Arjun Frueh, Kathy Gay, Greg Glass, Will Godwin, Dave Gordon, Susie Green, Michael H., Deb Haggerty, Sarah Hedges, Michael Heppell, Paul Hill, Cleve Hillman, J. Michael Howard, Paul Howey, Austin Isaacs, Brett Johnson, Dale Justice, Todd Karvenek, Greg Kuykendall, Vanna Land, Noah Landow, Tom Lane, Frank Lasik, Cris Lee,

John Lisenbe, Joshua Little, Dan Lively, Linda Lovely, Ryan Lucas, Dennis Maguire, Dennis Malfer, Brad Marsh, Patti Martin, Dave McCartney, Jack McClure, Andy McGee, Elaine McNally, Brian Medendorp, Merry Metcalf, Julie Meyer, Thom Michaels, John Mills, Eric Mohr, Michael Monahan, Leland Nellist, DJ Neunaber, Alison Newband, Dan Newcombe, Mike Nichols, David Norris, Amy Nylund, Ed Oates, Charles Paradelas, Gene Parker, Matthew Partrick, Willis Paul, Tammy Pickurel, Steve Pitcher, Linda Radke, Simon Ratcliffe, Susan Reese, Gary Reinbold, Stephen Roberts, Chris Rogers, Maria Rogstadius, Chris Roxburgh, Bob Ruff, Neil S, Glenn Sampson, Harry Saul, Dan Scott, Mark Sholund, Yuosiph Skowron, Avi Smith, Sheldon Smith, John Smith, David Somers, Gary Steinman, David Strickland, Gene Sullivan, Izar Tarandach, Marty Thompson, Capt. Bob Thompson, Neil Tomlinson, Jim Updike, Jeff Vandenbroek, Ben Varela, John Vermillion, Scott Vincent, Sharon Vreeland, Justin Walters, Michael Walters, Joseph Walters, Dave Webster, John Weisflock, Johanna Welton, Jay Wilhelm, Shawn Williams, Rick Williams, Rhonda Wolberd, Rob Wood, Bill Wood, Matt Wright, Carlos Wx, Richard Yaker, Thomas Yamamoto, Chris Zimmer, Joe , Thoss, and Lulu.

If you would like to see your name on the above list next time, be sure to register online at my website (theshipseries.com) or drop me a note at jerryaubin.author@gmail.com so I can put you on the list of readers to contact later in 2017 as Book Five approaches publication.

I would like to close by expressing tremendous gratitude for my family. My lovely and amazingly talented wife Kerry has provided constant encouragement and been supportive about the number of mornings I've spent building this world. My boys, Parker and Wesley, are always great sources of inspiration. Finally, Queso the wonder boxer is always available for a quick walk whenever I want to stretch my legs and clear my head after some gnarly piece of writing. Otherwise, she provides a helpful soundtrack of snorts and snores while she sleeps in her bed next to my favorite writing chair. You can follow her adventures on Instagram - @missqueso.

Made in the USA
Lexington, KY
06 September 2018